Hunting Beside the Loch

(A Cosy, Scottish Highland Mystery)

Abigail Shirley

DEDICATION

For anyone who has ever fallen in love with the magic of Scotland.

And for Jordan, who patiently listens to me talking about the lives of people who only exist inside my head.

'My heart's in the Highlands, my heart is not here,

My heart's in the Highlands, a-chasing the deer;

A-chasing the wild-deer, and following the roe,

My heart's in the Highlands, wherever I go.'

By Robert Burns

Glossary of Scottish Words

Aye – yes

Bairn – child

Blether – gossip

Brae – hill/slope

Braw – nice/brilliant/fantastic

Cannae – can't

Clarty – dirty

Dinnae/didnae – doesn't/don't/didn't

Dreich – gloomy/dull

Feart – scared

Ken – know

Laddie – boy

Lassie – girl

Och – an interjection of confirmation or affirmation and often disapproval

Peely-wally – pale and sickly

Wee – little

Widnae/wasnae – wouldn't/wasn't

Leaving England

August 2021

Walking out of the cubicle, I automatically make my way over to the sinks and start washing my hands. After pressing the tap down for the third time to rinse away the soapy water, I can't help but glance up at the mirror. There I stand, in blue jeans and a yellow T-shirt. My hair is pulled back into a ponytail. It's shining against the reflection in the glass like polished copper. Unlike my shining hair, my green eyes, surrounded by a circle of darkness, stare lifelessly back at me. They're peeping over the top of a black face-covering.

Standing on either side, also visible in the reflection of the long mirror which lines the rows of sinks, are two other women. Both of their mouths are clearly visible, unlike mine which is hidden safely behind its covering. One of the women is quietly smiling to herself whilst the other is holding her lips pressed together in a flat line. They both stand like twin towers either side of me, idly washing their hands. As usual, I'm the shortest woman in the room.

'*Little Laura*,' I whisper to myself.

That was what mother had always called me. Mother wasn't the only one who'd called me that though. The rest of the family did too for the first few years of my life. However, being half Scottish and growing up in Scotland, it wasn't long before I became known to everyone around me as, Wee Ginge. It's a description that actually suits me really well. My father used to love sliding words together and often the two words of my nickname would get shortened to, Winge. That's a less apt description of myself though because I've never been a moaner, despite the frustrations that tend to come with a lack of height.

Sometimes it's fun being just 5 foot and 1 inch in height. Like when you're at a festival and you get to sit on your mate's shoulders to watch your favourite band perform on stage. At other times it's no fun at all. Such as when you're trying to reach an item from the top shelf of the supermarket and there are no mates in sight to help you out.

Tucking a stray strand of hair behind my ears, I turn to make my way over to the hand dryer.

With a last, quick glance at the mirror, I can't help but let out a melancholy sigh.

'Little Laura looks tired,' I think to myself, silently.

Another woman walks out from a cubicle and passes by where I'm now standing, drying my hands. She too is not wearing a face-covering and, without thinking, I tilt my head to one side in an effort to distance myself from her. It's something that has become a force of habit over the past few weeks. Just last month, the rules regarding face-coverings in indoor, public spaces was relaxed by the English government.

'At least in Scotland everyone will still be wearing masks,' I reason and exit the ladies' toilets.

The motorway services at Penrith are already busy. Holiday-makers mill around everywhere. Their small, out-of-control children are running about and getting in the way as I try to navigate a route to the coffee kiosk.

Before pulling off the motorway, I'd been driving for over four and a half hours without stopping. That's a record for me. I usually need a toilet break within thirty minutes of setting off on a car journey. But then, I did leave at five o'clock this morning, which is a time of day when my bladder is normally sleeping.

It will probably be another five hours before I reach Inverness. I've decided that I need some caffeine.

Eventually, with a double espresso and a ham sandwich in hand, I'm able to make my way back towards where my car is parked and, upon getting into the driving seat of my Volkswagen Golf, I catch sight of my two suitcases. They're both weighing heavily on the back seat.

I have no idea why, but I rarely use my boot space. Instead, I prefer to pile everything onto the three empty seats behind me.

Reluctantly, I'd packed two cases instead of one after telling my boss that I hoped I wouldn't be away for too long. It was a half-truth: I really do hope that this trip won't take too long. But on the other hand, I honestly have no idea how long it's going to be before I'll be free to return to Oxford.

Oxford... it's become my home over the past twenty months. If I'm honest, it's become my escape, my sanctuary. The long weeks of lockdowns and restrictions passed by easily in that beautiful, historical city. If you'd have told me two years ago that I could be happy anywhere other than Scotland, I would never have believed you, but it's true, I've managed to find solace in the university city of Oxford.

There's no solace for me now though as I drive my car out of the services and rejoin the motorway to continue my journey northwards.

The coffee was, in fact, unnecessary. It was a mere precaution at best. In truth, there's no chance of me falling asleep. Sleep is something that has eluded me for months now. Instead, insomnia has become an uninvited and unwanted companion.

As my car passes the border and I find myself entering the country of my birth, my thoughts race back to the last visit I made to my homeland. It was just seven months ago, in January.

The whole of the U.K. had been in full lockdown at the time. Despite that, Andy's funeral was deemed a permissible reason for travel and so I had flown from London to Edinburgh and then taken the train into Inverness in order to attend the wretched occasion. Already distressed, my nerves were further tested by the risks of using both air travel and the public rail service during a pandemic. As a result, I'd attended the funeral, barely holding it together.

Cautious as always and mindful of the need to stick to the rules, I'd only stayed for one night, in a hotel next to the airport, before returning to England the following day.

The one moment I broke the law was at the crematorium. As I'd stood, watching whilst the curtain closed around my brother's coffin, I'd reached out and held on tightly to the hands of both my mother and my sister-in-law. It was a small piece of human contact that we all deeply needed in that moment, and I still believe it was the right thing to do.

A large Asda lorry now thunders past me as I'm skirting

around the outskirts of Glasgow, and it jolts me back to my senses. My mind had drifted and gone back to that night when I received the call that Andy had died.

The call had come from the police, a Detective Chief Inspector to be precise. Usually, people hear about the shocking news of a loved one's death from some other family member or even a close friend, but not me. No, I'd been told the news by a complete stranger. He was a kind stranger, and his soft, Edinburgh Morningside accent had been like honey to my ears, but he was still a stranger, nevertheless. The stranger's voice on the end of the phone told me that Andy had sadly died during a hunting session, earlier that evening. DCI Shaw broke the news gently and then waited politely for a few moments for his words to sink in. I'd sensed his waiting at the time but hadn't detected (no pun intended) the reason for it.

Once a sufficient amount of awkward silence had passed, he then got to the real purpose for his call.

'It would appear, under initial investigation, that your brother's death may not have been an accident. Miss McClintock, can you think of any reason why someone would wish to have your brother dead?'

I can remember that his question had hit me like a ton of bricks; *any reason?*

'No,' I told him, vehemently. 'None at all. Andy was loved by everyone. There wasn't a bad bone in his body. No one would ever want to kill him!'

And then Inspector Shaw had explained that there were five suspects in, what was now, their official murder investigation. The suspects were: Mr George Thompson, Mr William Mitchell, Mr Brochan

5

Henderson, Miss Ailish Briars, and Mrs Lilian McClintock.

'You're kidding?' I half-laughed in reply.

Silence was the only sound that had travelled through the phone.

As the names of those five people rang through my ears, I'd felt my head swish and my body sway from side to side. Reaching my hand out, I had taken hold of the side of the kitchen worktop in an effort to steady myself. *'This has to be a nightmare,'* I remember telling myself. But, of course, it wasn't a nightmare and just four weeks later, there I was at the funeral, in the presence of two of those suspects, one of whom had held onto my hand as tightly as I had held hers.

George Thompson, the gamekeeper of the Balnair Estate, near Inverness, looked at his watch and decided that it was time to call it a day. He was cold and the afternoon had been quiet. He'd been positioned at the top of the hill, just outside the woodland, on the edge of a large, open clearing which looked out across the Monadhliath mountains. George hadn't seen a single deer all afternoon. He was tired and now ready for some of Lily McClintock's homemade beef stew.

George unloaded his gun and packed it away. Picking up his bag, he then climbed down from his seat.

He'd only heard one shot so far that afternoon. It had rung through the air about thirty minutes earlier. It was hard up here, on the mountain, to detect the location of a gunshot. The sound of a bullet firing from its rifle was a noise which echoed all around, bouncing back and forth off the mountains.

'Broc,' he called on the radio. 'I'm making my way towards your seat now.'

Silence. The radios had been mostly quiet all afternoon.

George pressed the button on his radio, repeated himself and then waited a moment.

Still no response.

Never mind, George knew that he could approach Broc safely from behind. It was alright. Broc's seat was the closest to where he was. He would go there first and then they could walk back down to the others together. Something had seemed wrong with Broc earlier. George thought that the younger man had been rather agitated back at the house, before they'd all set out. Broc had snapped at Will, and his face had appeared troubled. George carried a hip flask with him. He would offer Broc a bit of fire for his

7

belly. That might cheer him up.

George carefully picked his way between the trees and after a few minutes he reached Broc's seat, but no one was there. Broc's bag and his radio were visible, up on the ledge, but there was no sight of the man himself.

From nowhere, the sound of a shot pierced through the air. It was loud and violent. Startled birds flew up into the sky and George jumped a little.

Should he carry on down to the others or should he wait?

George looked at his watch again… 3:55pm. He decided to wait a couple more minutes. If Broc had fired that first shot earlier, then he'd probably gone to trail after a running deer.

George didn't have to wait long. Just five more minutes passed before Broc appeared through the trees. He was slightly out of breath.

'George, you caught me,' he said, sucking in gulps of air. 'I'm not even able to walk uphill without struggling. I'm not as fit as I should be.'

The fifty-five-year-old gamekeeper smirked in response to the man who was twenty-three years his junior.

'Did you get one?' asked George, noting the barrel of Broc's rifle which was visible behind him as it sat in its sling around his shoulder.

'I wasn't sure at first, as it ran,' Broc answered him, reaching up onto his seat for his bag. 'Andy was with me though and he insisted we went after it. We found some blood and tracked it for a bit, but then we lost the trail over on the other side of the woods.'

'You know Andy,' smiled George. 'He likes his estate clean, not clarty.'

'I know, I know. Anyway, are you finished?'

'Aye. Where is Andy then, if he went with you?'

'We were right down the hill so he was going to check the

traps then make his way back to his seat,' explained Broc.

'I didn't hear either of you on the radios,' commented George as he watched Broc pick his radio up and put it into his pocket.

'I left mine here. Andy made sure to let you all know on his though. Although, the response was very crackly.'

George gave him a disapproving frown and then suggested they make a move. 'Shall we walk down to the others?'

Broc nodded and they set off, radioing though to the others that they were coming.

Ailish's voice came back to them. 'I'm packing up too. I just got one. I'll grab my stuff and go over to it once you all get here. It dropped immediately to the ground, so I must have made a nice clean shot.'

'Those girls will show us up with their perfect aims,' commented Broc, and George chuckled to himself in response.

George handed Broc the hip flask. 'Is there anything you want to talk about, laddie?' he asked kindly.

'No? Why do you ask?' replied Broc, keeping his eyes ahead and taking in a mouthful of the smoky liquid.

'Och, it's just you seem a bit…'

The end of George's sentence was drowned out by the crisp snap of another shot firing through the air.

'Another one,' said George. 'The deer must be moving. It's typical, isn't it? The wee beggars. They wait until we're all about to go home. It's like they know we're here some days, I'm sure of it.'

'We're losing the light fast now,' observed Broc. 'That will probably be it for the day. Andy told us to stop about now, didn't he?'

'Aye, we won't be getting any more today.'

About ten minutes later, they arrived at the bottom seat

where Andy and Lily had been set up. The light was now low and dusky. Will was there. He was talking to Lily, still wearing his ear defenders on his head. They were standing close together as they talked, and it startled them a little when Broc and George arrived. Lily looked up expectantly as they approached.

'Where's Andy?' she asked them.

Broc answered her, 'We tried to trail one but lost it, so I went back to my seat. He said he would make his way back here.'

'He's not returned yet.' Lily said, as Ailish also joined them from where she had been sat. 'And I've not heard from him on the radio,' Lily added.

'I think his radio isn't working that well,' said Ailish. 'When Andy got to me, I told him off for not radioing what he was doing, and he insisted that he had been doing so. Or maybe your radio isn't working?'

'Mine is fine, I've heard you and George talking, just not Andy, or Broc.' Lily frowned and turned her radio off and on. It seemed to be working properly. 'Anyway, never mind my radio. Does anyone know where Andy is?'

'He did say he was going to check one of the traps, further down the hill. He'll be back in a minute I expect,' said Broc. 'While we wait for him, shall we go and look at that deer you got Ailish?'

'I got one too,' interrupted Lily. 'That last one was me. Thankfully, I got a clean shot. Look... I'm still shaking. I always worry it's going to run off injured.'

Lily held her shaking hand out for them to see and Broc looked at George and smirked, 'What did I say earlier?'

George nodded. Broc was right. Both Lily and Ailish were good with their aims. It was impressive.

Broc turned his attention back to the two women. 'Okay, you first then Lily. Where is it?'

Lily pointed to an area which was up the hill from where

they were standing. It was a section of the forest where the woodland bushes were thicker.

'That's the same place where I hit mine,' said Ailish. 'I think there is a slight overlap in the target ground between our two seats.

'Well, if we get up there and only find one deer, you'll have to work out between yourselves who it was that made the winning shot,' teased Broc. 'Come on then, let's go and see, shall we? Leave your bags and things here if you want. I'll bring my gun.'

George looked across at Will. He'd been standing quietly at a distance, leaning against the bottom step of the high seat that Lily had been shooting from. As Broc, Ailish and Lily put their head torches on and set off though the woodland, George asked Will if he was going to go with them.

'No.' Will shook his head and wouldn't make eye contact. 'I'd prefer to stay here.'

George knew that Will could be a bit funny in his ways.

'Och, come on laddie,' encouraged the older man. 'I'll walk with you. We can stay behind the others. Come on, let's go with them.'

Will shook his head again and so George left him beside the seat, surrounded by everyone's gear, and followed the others.

They walked quite a distance to reach the area that Lily had pointed to. It was further away than it had looked. The others were still ahead and, as they approached the spot, George could tell from the excited, muffled voices that there was indeed a target on the ground.

Then, suddenly, the voices stopped. Seconds later, a loud piercing scream which was shortly followed by a shrieking wail of despair reverberated in George's eardrums and he found his feet running, as he stumbled through the undergrowth to get to where they were.

When George reached them, he looked down to see that Lily was bent low against the woodland floor. In the light from his head torch, he could see that she was shaking as she tried desperately to lift the lifeless body of her husband from the ground.

George wasn't a doctor, but he didn't need to be. It was quite clear to everyone: Andrew McClintock was dead.

Into Scotland

The traffic on the A9 is now beginning to get heavier so I flick the indicator to the right and join the stream of cars in the outside lane that are travelling a mere two or three miles an hour faster than the others. I can't help but notice that I'm passing camper van after camper van of various shapes and sizes. Some appear capable of housing entire families in positive luxury, while others look as though the owner's dirty work-tools might still be inside, along with a hand-pumped air bed and a cheap, portable stove. In front of me, is a heavily loaded car. It's full of people and belongings and a roof box carries even more of their stuff. The panting face of their dog is staring back at me from the rear window and it brings a smile to my face.

Since the onset of the Covid-19 pandemic and the lack of overseas travel, the good people of Great Britain have taken to exploring their own small island. Thanks to hashtags and shares across all the social media platforms, the 'North Coast 500' has become an experience that every Brit now wants to tick off their bucket list. It's for this reason that I now find myself driving alongside hundreds of others. Most of them are heading towards Inverness where the iconic route around the Scottish coast both begins and ends.

I sigh and turn on the radio. The presenter is talking about issues in Afghanistan and I quickly switch it over to a different channel. I need music, preferably something to which I can sing along. Driving in traffic is boring enough without listening to politics as well.

The last thirty seconds of Leona Lewis singing, 'Bleeding Love' plays out before it fades into OutKast's, 'Hey Ya'. Turning the volume up, I can't help but shake my hands 'like a Polaroid picture' whilst simultaneously balancing them on top of the steering wheel. It's not long before I'm singing along too. I can feel my spirits lifting. I love it when radio stations go all nostalgic. The track ends and I take a glance over at the passing scenery whilst awaiting the next song.

Adverts are playing and I remain patient. The station is running a 'songs of the noughties' session and I'm eager to know what will play next. While a tacky jingle announces some brilliant deal at a local furniture store, I notice that we're passing through some hills. The train of cars I'm travelling with is now skirting the edge of the Cairngorms. We pass by the junction for House of Bruar retail establishment, and I think back to the many trips we've taken there as a family to buy new hunting jackets or boots, or some other item of expensive clothing.

Before my thoughts can get too carried away, the adverts end and the next song begins. The voice of Tony Christie hits my ears and I once again start to sing along. As I'm shouting the chorus, 'Is this the way to Amarillo?' I find myself transported back to 2005.

It was my school leavers' prom and there I was, hanging onto the back of Ailish as we 'conga'ed' our way around the school hall with about fifty others.

The guy behind, who was almost ripping my dress off my body, had accidently stood on the back of my shoe and the heel nearly came off. I'd stumbled for a moment and then ran to catch up with Ailish, grabbing hold of her waist once again and leaving 'bigfoot' trailing far behind. She laughed as we both skipped along and kicked our legs out in time with the music.

The memory is a happy one, but it brings me back to reality with a forceful jolt.

I don't know if Ailish and I will ever have the same friendship again. After all, she had been there on that afternoon when Andy had died. She is still a suspect, even now, eight months later.

Reaching my hand out, with the smile gone from my face, I turn the radio off. The noise is now irritating my ears.

No. I doubt that things will ever go back to how they used to be.

Finally, I'm able to turn off the main drag and follow the B825, a single-carriageway road which snakes alongside Loch Ness. I could have turned off earlier and taken a more direct route home, but instead I've chosen to follow the A9 all the way to Inverness before heading towards the direction of Balnair. It's 10 miles longer to come this way, but at this point in the journey, it doesn't make much difference and besides, something deep inside has drawn me in this direction. My feelings about returning home have so far been a combination of apprehension and nerves, but both of those emotions are currently being overridden by a sense of nostalgia. I'll admit, it's surprising that I'm starting to feel a bit nostalgic, but it's also quite nice. It's giving me a warm, fuzzy feeling, and that's why I've gone out of my way to take this route home. This is a road that provides me with plenty of material for nostalgia.

By now it's gone 4pm. I've had another two toilet breaks

(thanks to the espressos) and eaten a sandwich. I'm feeling tired, but it's okay; I know the route well from here. My car purrs contentedly as it now travels along familiar roads.

Loch Ness, peeping at me through the trees to my right, is quiet. A few boats can be seen going up and down, but that's all. There are few places on this stretch of road to get to the shoreline and so the famous loch holds its eerie silence.

I've never seen 'Nessie'. Andy once claimed he spotted the monster from the window of the school bus on the way home one day. He wasn't the only one who said it and so I'm inclined to think that maybe he did see it. Do I believe in the Loch Ness monster? I don't know… the jury is still out for me.

I pass by the small village store at Foyers and hesitate briefly for a moment. It would probably be a good idea to pick up a few essentials: bread, milk, etc. But I can't face it. Not now. I have visions of being stared at, talked about and, most probably, questioned.

I can just imagine them all, huddled behind the shelves which hold packets of coffee granules and tubs of soap powder. *'Hush, look. It's her: Laura McClintock. Well, I never! We've seen nothing of her for months now. It must be true. His widow must have gone mad. Why else would his sister be here?'*

No, I can't deal with the villagers. Not just now.

Instead, I drive on, passing Cameron's Farm Shop which is already closed for the day. Only a few miles further down the road, just past Whitebridge, I take my last turn left and follow the single-track road up and into the hills.

The clouds are hanging low and my car is driving

through fine mists of midges. I shudder at the wretched beasts. There are a lot of things that I've missed about Scotland during my time away, but the midges are something I'll never miss. Thankfully the summer is almost over. Hopefully they'll soon be gone.

The narrow road I'm driving on winds its way around the hills and I look down at the river, flowing back in the opposite direction. I'm almost home. There's just one last hurdle to get past and then I'll be there.

As my car approaches the entrance to the Henderson's farm, I take in a deep breath and fix my eyes firmly on the road ahead. This is all hard enough without risking a sighting of Broc. The muscles in my neck start twitching as I fight against the urge to look up the driveway at his house.

I've never not looked before.

For as long as I can remember, each time I'd pass by, I'd always glanced sideways, hoping to see him. Hoping he'd look up from whatever he was doing and wave. But not now.

Not ever.

No, I will never look out for Brochan Henderson ever again.

28th December 2020

4.25 pm

It took George a moment to take in everything.

Broc had already grabbed hold of Lily and was trying to pull her to one side. Ailish was white, her face drained of all colour. George stepped forwards and reached out towards her. He caught hold of her as she fell, almost fainting, to the ground.

It was then that George realised he was shaking too. He stood up and switched on his head torch. The darkness of the night was rapidly engulfing the shadows of twilight and now was not the time for obscurity. George looked up towards where Ailish had been seated all afternoon. The beam of his torch located her high seat. About one hundred and fifty yards away, he estimated. He then looked back from where they'd walked. Lily's seat was a lot further away from them. More like three hundred and fifty yards, possibly more. In the low, evening light, it was no longer visible from where they all stood.

There was the sound of branches snapping and Will appeared beside them all.

'What is it?' he called, looking at Lily.

He then saw the body of his brother-in-law on the ground and his own face went white. Will ran over to his sister and tore Broc away from her, attempting to comfort her himself.

Broc walked over to George and stood beside him. He felt like his legs were about to give way.

'What should we do?' Broc asked the older man.

'We need to get the lassies away from here,' said George, snapping into action. 'William, help Mrs Lily to her feet and get her back to all our bags. Broc, let's help Miss Briars up.'

As Broc went over to help Ailish, George carefully scanned the area. It was overgrown with so many small bushes.

Andy's body was lying in a pool of blood and his brown hunting hat was still on his head. George needed to get back to his bag quickly, retrieve his phone and call the emergency services. As he moved, something caught George's attention.

About 20 yards away, just to the side of a smaller overgrown area, was another dark shadow on the ground. George went over to look. It was a deer. It had been cleanly shot and was also lying in a pool of blood. The two dead bodies were so close together.

Suddenly, Will began shouting and ran furiously at Broc. George turned around to see that Will was pounding Broc with his fists as he was trying to steady Ailish on her feet.

'It was you! It was you!' Will was shouting, angrily.

Lily had managed to stand up and was now trying to pull her brother away.

'Will! Stop it!' she cried.

'No! It was him. I saw him. He was down here earlier, wandering around without telling anyone. 'Andy wasn't with him. Broc's been in a bad mood all day. He did it. I know he did. He did it!'

Broc looked at George and their eyes met. Broc's were wide, bloodshot and tears were pouring from them. He stood still, shaking his head in confusion.

'I didn't shoot Andy,' he protested.

Will pulled himself free from Lily and ran off into the evening light, back towards the high seat where they'd left all their things.

Lily was now laying, once again, on the floor, sobbing loudly. Ailish had collapsed.

George looked again at Broc.

'I didn't shoot him,' Broc repeated. His voice was quiet.

It was cold and getting darker and darker as each minute

passed. George took in a deep breath. Whatever had or hadn't happened, he would need Broc on his side if he was going to get the two women back to the house.

'I need you to help me,' he said, and Broc nodded silently.

Between them both, George and Broc supported Lily and Ailish back to the high seat. When they arrived, there was no sign of Will.

George immediately found his phone and dialed 999. He walked away from the earshot of the others as he calmly explained to the operator their terrible situation.

It was with the relief of knowing that the emergency services were on their way that he returned to the others and told them they needed to all get off the hillside and back to the house.

The walk back home was long and slow. No one spoke. All of them were numb from what had just happened. The silence was only broken by the frequent sobs and sniffs of emotion escaping from each of them as the image of their beloved Andy remained burned in front of their eyes.

Returning to Balnair

Eventually, my car rounds the final bend in the road and Loch Balnair comes into view. I shudder as a ripple of emotion travels down my spine. Even against the moody, grey clouds our loch looks magical.

Yes, that's right, I did just say 'our loch'. This mile-long loch is part of the Balnair estate and therefore belongs to us: the McClintocks.

Pausing my car on the bridge that crosses the river, I look over to the loch. Mountains which form part of the Monadhliath range, rise majestically out of the water at either side and then disappear into the swirling fog. The surface of the water is still and calm. There's not even a ripple or a rise from the fish below. '*It's my loch now,*' I think to myself. I've loved this loch so much and for so long, but I'm not really sure that I want it, not under these circumstances.

Ignoring the many questions that are clawing at my mind, I ease my foot off the clutch and gently accelerate my car into our driveway.

Our family home is nestled amongst a small thicket of trees which hides most of it from view of the road. I drive past the front entrance, which always reminds me of a turreted tower from 'Sleeping Beauty', and make my way instead to the back of the house.

It's a fairly large house: eight bedrooms, three reception rooms and a large dining room, as well as a kitchen, study and numerous bathrooms. The building is nothing special to look at from the outside. Various additions and extensions have been built over the years.

It would appear that my ancestors had not been very good architects, as nothing seems to match. Perhaps that's why I love it so much; it's a bit higgledy piggledy. There's nothing ostentatious about the place as you might expect from a large, Highland Estate. It's a bit like us, the McClintocks: mismatched and humble.

As the wheels of my car come to a halt on the gravel, I hear a bark and an excited black Labrador comes bounding around the corner.

'Buddy!' I call, flinging the door open and bracing myself as he leaps into the car and onto my lap, his wet tongue attacking my face.

'Oh, I did miss you, old boy. Yes, yes, I did,' I say, ruffling his neck and patting him lovingly on the back. 'Come on, off you get. I need to get out.' I gently push Buddy away and climb out of the car. My legs and back feel stiff and so I take a moment to stretch before making my way over to the back door. I'll come back for my suitcases later. I need to see mother first.

The welcome from Buddy has momentarily brought me joy, but my body now trembles with emotion as I enter the house and call out nervously, 'Hello. I'm here.'

Within moments there is a sound of footsteps approaching. They're light and fast. Not Andy's, of course. And obviously not Lily's either. I wait until a woman in a medical uniform appears around the corner. It's one of mother's nurses.

'You must be Laura.' The other woman smiles at me from beneath her plastic face shield while holding out her arm.

'Hello,' I say and shake her hand.

It feels odd: almost as if I'm the guest and this is her home. But then, the three women we employ to care for our mother spend most of their lives in this house, so I suppose it sort of is like home for them.

'Julie?' I guess.

'Yes,' she smiles. 'Your mother is resting in her drawing room.'

'Is she awake?' I ask. 'If she is, I'd like to see her.'

Julie nods and I follow her down the hallway.

I suddenly realise that I'm shaking. I'm actually feeling nervous about seeing my own mother. It sounds ridiculous when I admit it now, but it's true; I am.

I quietly follow Julie into mother's small drawing room which is positioned just off the main family lounge. The windows face southwest and what little light there is behind the clouds is finding its way into the room. Over in the far corner, under the artificial light of a lamp, sits my mother. She looks thin and frail. Her hair, once thick and wavy, is now wiry and straw-like, hanging shapelessly around her jawline. She is staring absently at nothing. My poor mother is only fifty-four years old and yet she looks closer to sixty-five.

I fight back the tears which are threatening to escape as I approach quietly and sit beside her.

'Hello mother,' I say, taking hold of her hand.

She doesn't jump or flinch. Instead, she turns towards me and smiles.

'Ah, my dear, how lovely to see you.'

Her clear, English accent sings softly in my ears.

Mother had always been too delicate for the Highlands.

I look back at her and smile in return, fooled for a moment into believing that she knows who I am. She doesn't, of course. I could be anyone and she'd greet me in the same way.

True enough, her smile fades as a troubled look comes over her face and she turns her head in Julie's direction.

'Who is this woman?' she asks her nurse and I feel myself flinch as her words sting me hard.

Mother's mind is going, or rather, it is retreating. She no longer lives in the present but seems to be trapped in the past. I don't suppose that is necessarily a bad thing. My father and my brother are both still alive, in the past. To be honest, the past is probably a happier place to be. I envy her slightly.

Mother was first diagnosed with Early-Onset Alzheimer's five years ago. We'd all suspected it for longer though. Alzheimer's is something I'd always associated with old people. However, one day, I was reading through some of the disease's symptoms on a poster in the doctor's surgery and it dawned on me that the words in front of me gave an accurate description of my mother and her behaviour. The things she did and said, things we'd all just put down to her being a bit 'scatty' in nature, were actually a sign that something more sinister was going on, unseen to us all. After the diagnosis, mother's condition didn't change much initially. It wasn't until after my father had his heart attack and then two weeks later died, that she really began to deteriorate. By the time Andy and I buried our father, I realised that I'd already lost my mother to her pitiful disease. I felt like an orphan that day as I stood holding Andy's hand in the graveyard. Our mother was beside us both, declaring to everyone that she wasn't sure of who we were.

I feel helpless as I now wait, watching while Julie expertly calms mother down, telling her that I'm a friend who has come to visit. Now that she is settled, I sit for a few minutes and talk to her of things familiar to her. We speak about the old dogs which died many years ago and of her friends down at the golf club that she hasn't been to for years. After a while, I realise that I'm both tired and hungry, and so I give mother a kiss goodbye and head to the kitchen. I make myself a quick plate of beans on toast, taking note of the lack of provisions in both the cupboards and the fridge. Yawning, I then go back outside to the car to collect my cases.

It's now almost 7pm and it's still light, but it feels to me like midnight, I'm so tired. The midges are swarming and so I quickly pull the cases from the back seat and slam the door shut behind me. As I click the button to lock the car, I hear a cough from across the driveway. Looking up, I can see that it's Mr Thompson. He's standing against the trees and Buddy runs over to him instantly.

'George,' I call out and walk over to him.

'Miss Laura,' he replies and removes his cap politely. 'It's braw to see you home.'

I can't help but smile. George has known me since the day I was brought back from the hospital as a two-day-old baby in my mother's arms.

'It wasn't the easiest journey,' I sigh.

'No, I don't expect it was,' he nods. 'Still, you're here now.'

I smile again at him as he regards me with his kind, dark eyes. George's eyes sit upon wrinkled lines that have been etched into his skin from many years spent working outdoors in all weathers. George knows my emotions. He knows them because he also feels some of them himself. He's almost a member of the family.

'I'm sorry, I'm just so tired from the drive. I'm sure there's much I need to sort out, but can it all wait until tomorrow?' I ask, wearily.

'Aye, of course, Miss,' he replies and walks over towards my cases. He picks them both up and carries them to the back door.

'Sleep well, Miss. I'll be in my cottage if you need anything.'

George walks away and I head inside, closing the door behind me. Having him nearby makes me feel safe.

George Thompson is the only one of the five original suspects that has so far been removed from the list. I never thought for a moment that he should have been a serious consideration anyway. If there is anyone I can trust to look out for the best interests of the McClintocks, it's our George Thompson.

Police Interview Between Detective Chief Inspector Shaw (DCIS) and George Thompson (GT)

DCIS: Mr Thompson, would you like to take a break?

GT: No thank you. I'd prefer to get this done with as soon as possible. It's all very distressing.

DCIS: I understand. In that case, we'll continue. So, Mr Thompson, you said that you yourself fired no shots all afternoon, is that correct?

GT: Aye, that's right.

DCIS: And when did you last fire your rifle, before yesterday?

GT: It was Boxing Day, the 26th. Mr Andrew and I went out alone for a few hours.

DCIS: I understand that most often, rifles are 'zeroed' to check their accuracy, prior to going out for a shoot? Are you saying that you didn't do that?

GT: No, I didnae need to zero mine. My rifle was already still set up from the 26th. Nothing needed adjusting.

DCIS: Mr Thompson, we have on record that your rifle is the 'Blaser' that we now have in our possession, is that correct?

GT: Aye.

DCIS: And what ammunition do you use?

GT: Point 308.

DCIS: Can you please confirm for the record that apart from the three shots you've mentioned already, did you hear anything else that day?

GT: No, nothing at all. As I told you, the deer were very quiet.

DCIS: Did you see anyone else in the party moving about suspiciously or doing something odd?

GT: No. Brochan said he went to track the red that he shot, but the only person who said he would

27

	be moving about was Mr Andrew.
DCIS:	Was that usual behaviour on a hunting session or a stalk?
GT:	It would be normal practice to move on a stalk, but, no, it's not really normal when we use the seats. But he'd told us all at the start that he would be moving about. I think he wanted a chance to catch up with his friends.
DCIS:	I understand that strict safety procedures are followed when you're out hunting?
GT:	Very strict, aye.
DCIS:	Did you all follow the procedures?
GT:	Most definitely! It's a serious thing, is hunting. We follow the rules.
DCIS:	When was the last time you saw Mr McClintock?
GT:	Once we'd arrived at the North Woods. It would have been just before 2pm. I left him and Mrs Lily at the lower seat with William, and I then escorted the other two to their seats before finally taking up my own position at the top of the brae.
DCIS:	And when was the last time you heard Mr McClintock's voice on the radio?
GT:	That was about an hour later. He radioed through to say that he was heading over to Brochan's seat to see him.
DCIS:	So, just to confirm, the last time you heard the victim was a few minutes before 3pm?
GT:	Aye, that's correct.
DCIS:	What time did you hear the first gunshot?
GT:	It was five past three. I remember because I looked at the time.
DCIS:	Do you know who fired the shot?
GT:	No. The sound bounces everywhere in the

mountains. But later I saw Brochan returning from tracking his shoot that ran, so I presume it was him.

DCIS: Did Mr Henderson radio to say that he had fired the shot.

GT: No, the radios were silent after that.

DCIS: Okay. I'd now like to ask a few questions about the hunting party itself. Do you know all these young people well?

GT: Aye, fairly well.

DCIS: Are they all experienced with hunting?

GT: Mr Andrew and Brochan Henderson have been shooting since they were bairns and could only just walk. Ailish Briars picked it up as a teenager. She's got the best shot I've ever seen in a woman. The newest hunter is Mrs Lily, but she's been shooting regularly for the last nine months. I'd say she's become quite experienced in that time.

DCIS: Would you say that she is someone who might make a mistake in the way she loads her ammunition?

GT: Mistake? In what way?

DCIS: Would it be possible for her to load the bullets the wrong way, for example?

GT: Well, anything is possible I suppose, but Mrs Lily knows the correct way to load her gun. She's done it enough times. I widnae think she'd make a mistake unless she wasn't concentrating or something.

DCIS: What about William Mitchell? Is he an experienced hunter?

GT: Och, no. He can't shoot. He hates guns. He's feart of them.

DCIS: I see. Did you see him handle Mrs McClintock's

29

rifle at any point?

GT: No.

DCIS: If Mr Mitchell is afraid of guns and can't shoot, why was he there?

GT: Mrs Lily wanted some time with her brother. With all the restrictions we've been under, she's not seen him. That was why we used the seats and didnae do a stalk, to keep the laddie safe. I wasn't overly happy about the whole thing, but Mr Andrew insisted, so I agreed to it anyway.

DCIS: Mr Thompson, do you think it is possible that Mr Mitchell fired a shot at his brother-in-law and then deflected the blame to Mr Henderson.

GT: I'd say there was no chance of that at all.

DCIS: So, you think it could have been Mr Henderson?

GT: No, I dinnae... I didnae say that. What I'm saying is that there's no chance of young William shooting anyone. That laddie is more likely to get himself shot than to ever pick up a gun and shoot anyone.

DCIS: Why do you say that?

GT: He's just a liability. He gets a bit in the way. That's all. But like I said, he's proper feart of guns.

DCIS: Okay. Moving away from the subject of Mr Mitchell, I now need to ask a few questions about your personal relationship with Mr McClintock. How long have you been estate manager at Balnair?

GT: I've been manager for the last fifteen years. But I've been working on the estate for over thirty years, ever since I left school.

DCIS: Do you like working for the family?

GT: Aye, I do. They've been braw people over the years.

DCIS: And have you ever had any issues with Mr McClintock since he became the current Laird?

GT: No, none at all. He's... sorry, he *was* a good man.

DCIS: Can you think of anyone who would want to harm him?

GT: Like I said, he was a good man. Everyone loved him.

DCIS: What was his relationship with Mrs McClintock like?

GT: I've never known a couple more in love than they were.

DCIS: So, would you describe them as happy?

GT: With each other? Aye.

DCIS: And separately?

GT: Mrs Lily is quiet sometimes. She always has been. I have seen her very upset on a few occasions and I dinnae ken for what reason. However, I've never heard Mr Andrew raise his voice or say a harsh word to her.

DCIS: So, would you describe Mrs McClintock as happy or unhappy?

GT: I'd describe her as happy, but fragile.

DCIS: Has there ever been anything suspicious about Mr McClintock's life or business dealings that you know of?

GT: No. He was honest in everything... although, there is one thing, now you mention it.

DCIS: Yes?

GT: Some cash withdrawals from his account. They began a few months ago.

DCIS: How much money was withdrawn?

31

GT: One thousand pounds each time.

DCIS: And how often were the withdrawals?

GT: Once a month.

DCIS: What were they for?

GT: He didnae say. He widnae tell me. Just said it was something private.

DCIS: And you have no idea what it was?

GT: None.

DCIS: And how was his relationship with the others, his friends?

GT: As I said, everyone loved him.

DCIS: Did you think that anyone was behaving oddly yesterday, or didn't seem quite themselves?

GT: Miss Briars looked off colour.

DCIS: Do you mean unwell?

GT: Aye, and quieter than usual.

DCIS: Can you think why?

GT: No. It's been months since I've seen her at the estate. She's a close friend of Miss Laura's and just hasn't been around as much recently since Miss Laura moved away.

DCIS: Apart from Miss Briars, was everyone else acting normal?

GT: Umm

DCIS: For the record, Mr Thompson is hesitating. Mr Thompson, I need you to answer the question please.

GT: Something was bothering young Brochan. I could see it from the moment he arrived. But he widnae talk about it.

DCIS: Do you think that Mr Henderson had an upset with Mr McClintock?

GT: Och, I widnae say it was that. Those two were close, like brothers really. They loved each other.

DCIS: Apart from thinking that something was bothering Mr Henderson, was there anything else not right about him or his actions.

GT: He didnae reply to me on the radio at the end of the afternoon and he wasnae at his seat when I got there. Turns out that he left his radio there too.

DCIS: Where was he?

GT: As I said earlier, he'd gone to trail a deer he'd shot and Mr Andrew had gone with him. Brochan returned to his seat not long after I got there.

DCIS: Do you know what time he returned?

GT: Aye. He came back at 4pm.

DCIS: Was he alone?

GT: Aye. He said that they'd lost the trail and that Mr Andrew had gone back to his own seat.

DCIS: Did either Mr Henderson or Mr McClintock radio through to tell you and the others that they were going after a deer?

GT: No. Brochan told me later that he'd rushed away from his seat and left his radio there. He said they'd used Mr Andrew's, but I never heard it.

DCIS: Don't you think that sounds a bit suspicious, Mr Thompson?

GT: Not really. I widnae describe it as suspicious.

DCIS: How would you describe that sort of behaviour then?

GT: Well, err. I'd say it was a wee bit careless.

DCIS: Is Mr Henderson normally a careless sort of person?

GT: No, quite the opposite.

DCIS: And yet, you still don't think his actions to be suspicious?

GT: No. Perhaps it's just a bit out of character.

DCIS: In my experience, when something is 'out of character' it's suspicious. Mr Thompson, did you see Mr Henderson and Mr McClintock together at any point that afternoon?

GT: No.

DCIS: I think that concludes the interview. Thank you for your help, Mr Thompson. We'll need to suspend your license until the forensics come back on your rifle, I'm afraid.

Facing the Village

The sound of running water causes me to stir in my sleep. Opening my eyes, it takes me a moment to work out where I am. Then I remember; I'm in Scotland. I'm at Balnair, but I'm not in my own room.

The previous night, when I brought my cases upstairs to go to bed, I walked down the hallway to my old room and opened the door. It looked different. My old bedroom is located next to Andy and Lily's room, and it looked as though they had made good use of it in my absence. Numerous items belonging to them had now found a home there. Having decided not to disturb their things, I closed the door and then turned around to see the open doorway to mother's room opposite. It had all been too much to take in at the end of a long day: Andy gone, Lily not here and mother so ill. I retreated back to the staircase and chose a room off the opposite hallway in which to set myself up for the duration of my stay.

All the rooms on this side of the house are guest rooms and we're not expecting any guests, so it doesn't matter where I choose to sleep.

I now turn over, onto my back, and listen again to the water. The window of my flat in Oxford is roughly the same distance from the river as is the window in this room. I lay, looking at the ceiling and think of the river Thames and how it flows silently though the city. In summer, visitors gracefully punt along the water. There

35

is something sedate and tranquil about it all.

The river I can now hear is running fast. In fact, it's sprinting past our house. No doubt, if it were as wide and deep as the Thames, then people would come from all around to kayak its fast flowing, white waters. It's wild: much like the Highlands around me.

Getting out of bed, I realise that I've slept through the entire night without waking; not once. That hasn't happened since the night I received the call from Inspector Shaw.

Feeling unusually refreshed, I take a shower, unpack my clothes into the small wardrobe and then head downstairs to have some breakfast.

As I reach the bottom step of the staircase my phone pings in my pocket. Pulling it out and checking, I can see that it's a WhatsApp message from one of my colleagues, Angela.

'Och aye lassie, did you get there safely?'

I smile and tap out a reply to her. She's a nice girl. Angela is five years younger than me, but she's really reached out and has proved to be a good friend since I arrived in Oxford. With the country going into lockdown just ten weeks after I moved, I didn't have much chance to meet people and we've become close over the past few months.

Buddy patters his way towards my feet and nudges against my leg, implying that he needs some food. I take the hint and walk through to the kitchen, pocketing my phone.

'Well, there's good news and bad news,' I announce, closing the cupboard doors and glancing at Buddy who is watching me expectantly. 'There's food for you, but there's nothing for me.'

Buddy lets out a whine and holds his paw out. I think he understands me.

I dish Buddy's breakfast up into his bowl and then reluctantly go to get my car keys and trainers. I may have put it off yesterday, but there's no hiding from it today; I need to pop to the village store. Ideally, I should go to Tesco in Inverness, but I don't want to drive that far, not after the long journey yesterday. I will see to a bigger shop later in the week.

Reaching my hand to the hooks where all the keys are kept, I catch sight of Andy's keyring hanging there, next to mine. Wondering for a moment if anyone has started his car recently, I make a quick decision. Snatching his keyring off the hook, I head outside and make my way to the yard where all the vehicles are parked. As I click the fob the lights on Andy's Defender flash and the doors unlock.

Don't get too excited. Andy's car is nothing fancy. 'Eileen', as Andy affectionately named her, is an old Defender. An '04' plate to be precise. She's as much a part of the family as Buddy is.

Stupidly, I fumble around for a moment with the keys, forgetting that the ignition is on the left side of the wheel, before finally putting my foot on the clutch and closing my eyes.

'*Come on Eileen,*' I whisper under my breath, smirking a little as that familiar, classic song comes into my head.

I turn the key and the system beneath Eileen's bonnet begins to turn over. Anxiously, I hold my breath. Will she start? Then, a small squeal of delight escapes from my mouth as her TD5 engine lets out a growl and she bursts into life.

'Good girl,' I say, patting the dashboard affectionately

and with that, we make our way out of the driveway.

It's a beautiful day. The clouds from yesterday have disappeared and everything is sunny and bright. I rumble my way along the road (ignoring again the entrance to Broc's place) and head down the hill to Foyers.

It's amazing how the light from our sun can affect one's mood. Yesterday, after the long drive and then walking into the house for the first time since it all happened, I'd felt very low. I'd even been close to tears as I'd struggled with the flurry of emotions that the day had presented to me. Now though, with the sun in my eyes and blue skies ahead, I can feel myself smiling a little. It's as though I've been injected with a tiny dose of happiness to help me face the grim reality that surrounds me.

Once at the village store, I quickly and quietly collect together some essential items and pay for them. The wonderful thing about wearing a face-covering is that very few people realise who is underneath. Leaving the store and walking down the steps, I'm congratulating myself on completing the whole exercise without any drama when I unfortunately commit the fatal mistake of making eye contact with the woman who is walking towards me.

Mrs Tweedle's hand instantly reaches out and grabs hold of my arm.

'Och, well! If it isn't wee Laura McClintock. What brings you home lass? Och, of course, it'll be because of poor, wee Lilian.'

I try to fill my head with polite pleasantries whilst simultaneously fighting the urge to roll my eyes and let out a huge sigh.

'Hello, Mrs Tweedle. It's nice to see you.' I reply, hoping that a small, white lie won't make me wicked.

I hover on the steps, holding my two bags of shopping, one in each hand, and graciously ask her how her grandchildren are getting on.

She responds to my enquiry, 'Blah blah, something blah...' I'm not actually listening. I don't want to be here. And then she says it. She asks the very question I've been dreading.

'So, they still haven't found the murderer yet then, I suppose?'

'*Murrrderrrerrrr.*'

Mrs Tweedle's tongue lingers against the roof of her mouth as she rolls her Rs, making that awful word sound more ferocious than needed. It echoes around my head.

Twenty months of living in England has heightened my amusement of certain expressions and phrases that us Scots tend to use. Right now, it means that the accent of my birthplace is suddenly alien to me.

'No. It would appear that a *murrrderrrerrr* is still running around on the loose!' I reply, rolling my own Rs sarcastically in return.

'Now, I'm sorry, but I must go. These bags are heavy,' I say, as I turn around and stomp angrily back towards Eileen.

28th December 2020

10:15 am

Laura McClintock's phone rang, vibrating against the kitchen worktop. It was a facetime call from Andy. She smiled. Turning the hob off and moving the frying pan of bacon rashers to one side, she picked the phone up and answered it.

'Hey you!' she said, holding the phone up in front of her face.

Her brother's big, beaming smile stared back at her on the screen.

'Wee Ginge! What are you up to? You look like you're still in your PJ's.'

'Of course I am!' Laura replied. 'It's the holidays. I don't get out of bed before 10am during the holidays, remember?'

'Oh aye, I remember well,' he laughed. 'And I bet you're cooking bacon too!'

She turned the phone to face the frying pan and they both laughed.

'What are you both up to?' Laura asked, turning the phone back towards her face and sitting down at her small dining table.

'We're going shooting later,' Andy paused. 'Broc and Ailish are coming over for it.'

Laura pouted. 'Just like old times,' she said, trying to smile.

'I know' Andy replied. 'It won't be the same without you.'

'It wouldn't be the same even if I was there,' she replied. 'The old days are gone. Things have changed.'

'No, they haven't.'

'Well…I have.' Laura glanced away from the screen.

'I do wish you were here,' he said.

'I know, I know,' Laura sighed. 'Best laid plans and all that. Anyway, are the others allowed to be there? I thought everyone was under restrictions. In England we have this tier system.'

'Yeh, same thing here really,' said Andy. 'We can't meet up indoors and can only see six outside. That's why we thought a hunting session would be good. We can all see each other without breaking the law.'

'I presume George is going? It would have been six exactly if I'd been there.'

'Yeh, we're taking Will instead.'

'Will?' questioned Laura, 'But he hates guns and loud noises!'

'He's missed not seeing us,' said Lily, her face appearing on the screen next to Andy's.

Laura smiled at the sight of her sister-in-law, with her beautiful, porcelain complexion and perfectly-neat, blonde hair.

'Hey Sweetie, how are you?' asked Laura, waving at her sister-in-law and opening her arm out in a virtual hug.

'I'm frantically trying to get a beef stew into the slow cooker,' replied Lily, waving an oxo cube in the air. 'Andy thought it would be a good idea to tell everyone that we can light the firepit and eat stew in the garden together when we get back later.'

'Sounds like most of my brother's good ideas. They're great, especially if someone else can execute them!'

'Exactly!' agreed Lily, poking playfully at Andy's cheek. 'Look, I'd better get on with this. I'll call you later, or tomorrow maybe.'

'Have fun!' called Laura, as Lily disappeared. 'She sounds chirpy. How are things?'

'Good,' said Andy, walking into another room and moving his mouth closer to the phone in order to talk at a quieter level. The camera faced his head and Laura stared at a small bald patch in his auburn hair as he continued talking, 'She's been a lot more relaxed since we spoke to the doctors. They assured her that we're still both young and, even if there are fertility issues, there's no need to worry as there's still lots of time to investigate other options.'

'I can see on her face that she looks happier.' Laura paused. 'How's mother?'

'She's not too bad. That new nurse started last week, the one we interviewed at the end of November. I think I sent you her C.V.'

Laura nodded. 'Does mother like her?'

'She seems to, so that's good.'

Laura bit her lip. 'I really need to try to get home at some point, don't I?'

'Och, don't worry. We have it all under control. Just as long as you're happy, it's all fine.'

Laura looked out the window. A pair of swans were pecking at the riverbank below.

'I am happy,' she told him.

'Good.'

Andy scratched his chin thoughtfully. 'Have you err… have you spoken to Ailish recently?' he asked. His head was once again bent over the phone and his voice quiet.

'No.' Laura let out a guilty sigh. 'I've been rubbish at keeping in contact with anyone to be honest. But thanks for the reminder, I'll have to try and call her next week. Can you give her my love? Tell her I miss her?'

Andy nodded, 'Aye, I will do.' He hesitated for a moment and Laura waited for him to say whatever was clearly on his mind.

There was a noise and Andy looked over his shoulder. 'Look, I've got to go over a few things with George before the others arrive. I'll have to go. We'll send you photos and stuff.'

'Have fun!' Laura called.

Putting the phone down, she went back to the hob and continued frying the bacon.

Going Over (the) Business

Arriving home from Foyers, I return Eileen to her space in the yard and get out. I'm feeling flustered, irritated and, to be honest, a bit upset. People give no consideration to the feelings of others sometimes before they open their mouths and speak.

I carry the bags of shopping into the kitchen and pop four croissants into the oven. Locating the cafetière, I spoon in two heaped dessert spoons of Italian ground coffee and let it infuse in boiling water for a moment.

Waiting for the coffee and its pot to do their thing gives me an opportunity to wander through and see mother. She's in her drawing room, sitting at a small table, eating her own breakfast. Mother's nurse is on a seat beside her, reading a book quietly. It's not Julie. The shift must have changed early this morning. I go over and say hello. Her name is Katrina.

Mother looks at me blankly as I lean down and kiss her good morning. She then asks me a simple question.

'Where is Caroline? I haven't seen her for a day or two.'

Caroline, mother's younger sister, lives in Australia and has been there for the last thirty-five years. I tell mother that Caroline is on holiday and will hopefully be back in a week or two. I've learned from listening to the tales that Andy would relay, that it is best to go with whatever period of time mother's head is in, rather than try to correct her, as it causes less upset and confusion.

Katrina nods at me approvingly and I feel assured that I've said the right thing, as wrong as it feels saying it.

Returning to the kitchen, I plate up a tray with the croissants and two cups of coffee, then make my way across the yard to George's small office.

Using my foot to gently knock against the door, I'm grateful when he opens it immediately and takes the tray from my hands.

'Och, Miss Laura, you didnae need to get me anything,' he says, smiling kindly.

Without a word, I step inside and sink in a small armchair next to George's desk.

'Mmmm,' I groan, lifting a warm croissant to my mouth and enjoying the flaky, buttery pastry.

'Did you go into Foyers for these?' asks George.

'Yes,' I reply. 'And I ran into Mrs Tweedle with her nosey nose.'

'Aye, well, that's Mrs Tweedle for you. She's always blethering about something,' he says, slurping on his coffee.

We eat our breakfast in silence and then, once finished, I sit upright and lean on the desk.

'So, what do you need me to sign and authorise?'

George is our estate manager. He's worked for us for years. Father took him on as gamekeeper not long before Andy was born. He is still the gamekeeper but has gradually taken on more responsibility over the years. I don't know what we would have done without him after father died. He handled everything so well for us all. It was a relief to have him and to know that we didn't need to worry about things. After father's death, both Andy and I were added as signees on the estate, even though it was Andy who inherited everything. Andy then added Lily after they were married. At the

45

time I didn't see what use it was me still being one, but now it would appear to have been a good decision.

There isn't as much to go over as I thought there was going to be, and we are done in about twenty minutes.

'There must be more than this to sort out, surely?' I ask, skeptically.

George nods. 'Aye. There is more and some decisions will need to be made, but it can wait for a week or two.'

'Can we still afford mother's care?' That's my main concern regarding the finances of the estate.

'Aye. That is all in order. No need to worry about that.' George gives me a reassuring smile.

Satisfied, I get up to leave and then hover for a moment with my hand on the door handle. George looks up at me expectantly.

'Is everything alright, Miss Laura?' he asks.

I let out a sigh. I've been wanting this moment, alone with George, for months and now I'm not sure if I'm ready for it.

'Do you mind if I ask you some things about...it all?' I eventually manage to say, shaking my hands out to relieve the tension I'm feeling inside.

George smiles again, that kind, wrinkly smile of his, and indicates towards the chair.

'Do you want to sit back down?'

With a nod I go back over to the chair and sit down.

'What do you want to ken?' he asks. His voice is calm and soothing. 'Didnae the police tell you most of it?'

'Yes,' I reply. 'They told me all the facts. I was just wondering... well, what I want to ask is... what do you think happened?'

I watch as George leans back in his own chair and drops his eyes to the floor. He pauses for a moment, thinking silently to himself. I force myself to be patient and wait for him to gather his thoughts. After a moment, he looks back up at me.

'I've asked myself that question over and over again,' he answers me. 'And still, I cannae work it out.'

George's eyes watch me, steadily analysing my reaction, and I try not to blink as my mouth forms the next question.

'Do you... do you think that Broc did it?' My mouth feels dry. I'm forced to run my tongue around the inside of my gums to try and create moisture in there.

'Brochan Henderson... murder his best friend?' George shakes his head. 'I cannae see it myself.'

I realise that I'm holding my breath.

George keeps talking. 'But young William saw it, or so he says he did.' George smiles at me sadly. 'The only thing I ken, is that three shots were fired that afternoon. Three people said that they hit a deer, but one of those shots didnae hit any deer.'

George's face has gone white, and I feel like mine probably has too.

'Has there been any more information about the cash that Andy seemed to be withdrawing?' I ask.

'No, I still dinnae ken what that was for. I asked him once, just two weeks before it all happened, and he told me it was something private. Told me not to worry about it.'

'It's strange.' I say, pondering it all. 'Has Lily ever spoken to you about the whole thing?'

George shakes his head.

As I sit watching George, a flicker of distrust crosses my mind. I've never been the sort of person to question someone's word, especially not the words of a man I've trusted my whole life. Distrust is a feeling I'd never experienced until the night that Andy died, but now I doubt everything and everyone.

I carefully study George's face, looking for any small hint of deception, but I can't see any. Shaking my head, I tell myself, '*No Laura. This is George. He wouldn't tell you a lie. Besides, the police have ruled him out of the investigation.*'

I decide to ask a different question.

'How was Lily? I mean, I know she's clearly lost it, but over the last few months, how was she coping?'

'She's been up and down. Clearly, she's a woman in deep grief and she misses your brother hugely, but you know Miss Lily better than us all; she's always been fragile and fretful. Always a bit peely-wally, you know?'

I do know. Lily is someone with (what a Victorian doctor would call) 'a delicate constitution'. Life has never been free and easy for Lily. It's no surprise she has ended up where she is now.

I stand up again to leave and then one more question comes to my mind.

'Do you think Lily knew what Andy was doing with that money?' I ask.

George shakes his head. 'No, Miss. I dinnae think so.'

Remembering the Second Phone Call from DCI Shaw

It was a few weeks after Andy's death, on a Friday afternoon, when my phone had rung, and I again heard the voice of Inspector Shaw talking to me.

'Miss McClintock. I thought you may like to hear an update on the investigation,' he'd said after greeting me formally.

'That's very kind of you,' I'd replied, trying as best I could to sound casual. The truth was, I'd been waiting anxiously for news from him for days.

'I wish I could give you a definite answer about what happened to your brother,' he said. 'But, sadly, we're not able to yet. Not at this stage, at least. One thing we have been able to do with certainty, is establish that Mr Thompson did not kill your brother. He has been removed from the list of suspects.'

'Oh.' My reply was short as I took in what he was saying to me. I'd never thought that George would have done anything like that anyway. What was shocking to me was that it was George, and George alone, who had been removed from the list. Surely the police didn't still think the others capable of murder?

'So does that mean that you still think one of the others did kill Andy?' I asked, trying to control the shaking in my voice.

'I'm afraid so,' he replied. 'We've been able to eliminate Mr Thompson on two grounds. Firstly, and most importantly, forensics have confirmed that his rifle was not fired that day.'

He paused and I asked the question that was foremost in my mind, 'Does that mean that the other three rifles were fired then?' I'd received very little information about what had happened that day. I hadn't spoken to either Broc or Ailish, and Lily couldn't seem to tell me anything. I'd felt quite hopeless, really. I was hundreds of miles away and completely in the dark about everything.

'Yes. That's correct,' Inspector Shaw confirmed.

'And what's the second reason?' I asked, curious now to know more.

'Motive,' he said. 'Mr Thompson simply has no motive.'

I remember that my breath caught in my throat and for a moment I thought I would choke.

'Miss McClintock? Are you still there?'

Somehow, I regained control of my breathing. 'Yes. Yes,' I answered him. 'I'm sorry Mr, err, Inspector, are you telling me that the others do have motive?'

I could tell from the intake of air that I heard on the other end of the phone that he was trying to think of the best way to answer my question.

'Yes,' he replied. His voice was quieter and almost sounded apologetic. 'For one reason or another, there could be a reason for motive for the others.'

'All of them?' I pushed.

'Yes.'

I closed my eyes for a moment.

'Do you mean to tell me that you have reason to believe that my brother's best friends, his brother-in-law, and even his own wife had motive to want to kill him?' My ears felt swishy, and I quickly sat down.

'When we use the word 'motive' we mean a reason to snap, a reason to react in a way that could result in something like murder,' he began to explain. 'People often think of motive as a pre-meditated, deep-seated issue over something, but often it can result from the smallest of upsets.'

'But even small upsets: Andy didn't really have those,' I insisted. 'Not with any of us lot at least.'

Inspector Shaw didn't respond.

'You think that there were small upsets?' I asked.

'Yes. Something wasn't right that day, and it would seem that each of the remaining suspects had reason to be upset over something.'

There was silence between us as I took in what he was saying.

'The forensics have eliminated George,' I said suddenly. 'Couldn't forensics tell you who did it?'

'They could, if we had a bullet,' he replied.

I've been hunting my whole life. I know that most often, with a clean shot, the bullet from a rifle passes straight through its victim leaving only an entry wound, an exit wound and a lot of damage in between. Bullets, whole or fragmented, are almost impossible to find.

'I take it you've searched for it?' I questioned, knowing full well what the response would be.

'We have,' he confirmed. 'This is a large woodland, where your family hunt regularly. We have found a lot of things, but nothing that we can use to definitively answer your question.'

I understood what he was saying. It would be like looking for a needle in a haystack; a haystack that was huge and also full of pins, tacks and other needles.

I went back to something which had been going over and over in my head since that fateful day.

'Inspector Shaw. My first thought when you called me that evening was that there had been an awful accident. Are you still so sure this isn't what happened?'

I don't know why, but I found myself hopeful as I asked him the question. As if it would be better to kill a beloved friend or family member by accident rather than on purpose. As I waited for his response, I realised that neither option would be good. Both were equally horrific.

'Mr Henderson, Miss Briars and Mrs McClintock are all experienced hunters,' he said.

'Yes,' I agreed.

'And they all follow a strict standard of safety when they hunt.'

I knew what he was saying. It was true: hunting was not a game and rifles were no toys. It was serious, and each and every one of us follow the rules when we are out.

'But even so,' I pleaded, 'Accidents do still happen, don't they?'

'Yes, they do,' he conceded. 'Accidents can definitely happen.' He paused before adding, 'But accidents among experienced, conscientious hunters are very rare. Sadly, in my job, I find that, more often than not, accidents don't just happen. Miss McClintock, none of the suspects have admitted to making a mistake. If an accident happens, that is usually what we hear: an admission of guilt.' His voice was now diplomatic. He was telling me something he knew I didn't want to hear. 'Until we get to the bottom of this, we are assuming that anything is possible and that includes murder. The fact is, someone's story isn't right. We need to work out who's story is wrong and why.'

I remember blinking as my eyes lost focus for a moment. I dropped my head into my hands.

'Are you telling me that one of them is lying?'

There was a pause.

'Yes,' he replied. 'That is exactly what at least one of them is doing.'

28th December 2020
10.30 am

'Sorry to disturb your phone call with Miss Laura, but I just wanted to go over everything for this afternoon.' George pulled out a plan of the estate and placed it on the table.

'Lily really wants Will to come with us,' said Andy. 'Over the past few months, she's not been able to see him much and she feels bad about that.'

'You know I'm not happy about it, but if you insist, then we'll have to make it work. What do you suggest?'

'I don't want to complicate things by doing a stalk. Especially as Will can be a pain if he's scared. I was thinking we could head over to the North Woods and just use the high seats up there. It would make everything much safer.'

'You know that I think a stalk would be far more advantageous, but that sounds like an acceptable idea for a compromise,' said George, looking closely at the map. 'The only thing is, there are only four seats on the brae.'

'I've thought about that. You, Broc and Ailish can take one each,' said Andy, pointing to different spots on the map. 'I'll share with Lily. It will give me a chance to move about a bit after a while and see the others. The main reason for this afternoon isn't the deer, it's basically an excuse to socialise.'

'Aye. Between you, me and Miss Lily, we've culled our fair share over the past two months. Soon we won't have any deer left on the estate for the visitors to shoot,' joked George. 'The freezers at the farm shop down the road are full though.'

'We've not had a lot else to do with all these blasted covid restrictions. Mind you, Lily's aim is pretty spot on as a result.'

'Aye,' smiled George. 'She'll out-shoot you in target practice before long.' George looked back at the map. 'And young William?'

'He'll stay with Lily and me. He can sit at the bottom of our seat. He won't move, he's too scared to.'

'Sounds braw,' said George, folding up the map. 'What time are the others arriving?'

'They'll be here for midday. We can all have a wee dram then walk up to the seats together.'

The Pile of Unopened Letters

I leave George in his office and take the plates and mugs back to the kitchen. Buddy is laid out in his bed and looks up at me as I walk in. His tail thumps against the floor but he doesn't bother to get up. I don't blame him. I don't feel like I'm the best company.

To be honest, I'm feeling extremely fractious and unsettled. The hours spent sitting in the car yesterday have stiffened my body and now my head is all a jumble too. I need to do something: something to clear my mind. If I was in Oxford, I would take my bike out for a ride around the city.

It's something I've come to love, riding around on my bike. My bike is nothing special. I'm scorned at by the Strava athletes who often pass by on their light, carbon-framed skeletons of a bicycle. No, my bike is old, heavy and even a bit rusty in places, but I love it anyway.

Oxford is the city of bicycles. They out-number cars. Within my first week of living there I'd purchased my bike and attached a small basket and a traditional little bell. During the first lockdown, I went out riding every day. To begin with, I'd stayed within the city, but then, as I got fitter and my legs got stronger, I ventured further and further afield. The countryside surrounding the city is beautiful. Large fields of steady rolling hills and hedgerows stretch as far as the eye can see. One day, I even went as far as Blenheim Palace, with a small picnic in the basket. The sun was shining and the birds were singing. I remember feeling happy that day.

But, here at Balnair, I don't have a bike and don't fancy riding the mountainous terrain either. I look out the window and notice that the sun is still shining. The air had felt warm when I crossed the yard from George's office. Stretching my arms above my head, I come to a decision; I'm going to go for a swim in the loch.

Running up the stairs, I make my way to my bedroom: my actual room, not the guest room I slept in last night. There'll be some swimwear in one of the drawers.

I open the door and step into the room. Although a lot of Andy and Lily's things are dotted around, the bedroom is still pretty much how I left it, twenty months ago.

I go straight over to my chest of drawers. On top are about a dozen frames, all containing photos. My eyes settle on the largest frame. Inside it is a photo from Andy and Lily's engagement party.

We were all there: 'the gang'. I can remember the picture being taken. Their party had been here at the house, and we'd all gone out to the loch for some photos. The sun was just setting behind the mountains and we were all cast in shadows. Despite that, you can see that we are all smiling. Andy and Lily are in the middle. He's holding her in his arms, as if about to step over some threshold. To the side of Lily is Will. He's not looking at the camera but is watching me whilst also holding one of Lily's feet in the air. I'm there next to Will, raising my glass of champagne up towards the cameraman with a triumphant grin on my face. My short blonde hair, as I wore it back then, is catching what few rays of sunlight are reaching the tops of our heads. On the opposite side of the photo, next to Andy, is Broc. His face is mischievous, and he looks as though he's trying to pinch the back of Andy's legs. Lastly, standing beside Broc, is Ailish. Her smile is not quite as strong as everyone else's, but she looks happy enough with her eyes fixed on the camera lens.

I run my fingers along the glass of the photo frame and a wave of sadness sweeps over me. We were an inseparable group of friends for so many years, but now it's all changed. The suspicions and uncertainties of what really happened that day have pushed us all apart. Lily is the only one I've spoken to since Andy was killed. My eyes stare at all our happy faces and I wonder, once again, if anything will ever be the same as it used to be, or will the wounds remain open forever? Will we all now go on living separate lives, occasionally thinking back to a group of people who had at one time meant everything to each other?

I pull my attention away from the photo and open the top drawer to look for my swimming costume. Eventually, reaching the bottom drawer, I locate the plain, black-lycra piece of clothing and pull it out. Underneath is a small pile of envelopes. Frowning, I pick them up.

There's half a dozen of them, all with the name 'Lil' on the front.

I think it a bit odd, as Lilian's name is only ever shortened to 'Lily' and I've never heard anyone call my sister-in-law, 'Lil'.

I turn the envelopes over. They are all sealed, except for one. Thinking it strange that Lily would store unread letters in the bottom of my chest of drawers, I go to put them back where I found them.

Something stops me though. It's my nosey curiosity, no doubt. I put the five unopened ones to one side and hold the open envelope in my hand.

It's wrong, I know, to read someone else's letter but something is eating at me to look at it.

Guiltily, I close the door to make sure no one can see me and go over to the window where it is lighter.

I slowly pull the paper out from the envelope and unfold it. It's a letter to Lily. There's no date. The handwriting is neat. It definitely isn't Andy's. His writing had been scrawling and hard to decipher. I read the letter silently to myself.

Dear Lil,

I can't believe you don't live here anymore. I can't believe you moved away and left me.

You told me that you needed to go and that you would be happy but I don't think you will be.

I saw you crying and I know why too. I know that he made you cry. He made you sad. I don't know why you love him. I love you Lil. I can make you happy. I can look after you. I wish you would come back home.

Love

B

I can't help but stare out the window, confused by it all. Who is 'B'? I wonder for a moment if this could be some sort of love letter from Broc to Lily and my heart pounds hard against my chest as I process that possibility. But no, that doesn't make sense. Even if Broc is secretly in love with Lily, she's never moved away from him. And so, she can't move back to him. To my relief, I realise that the letter must be from someone different. But I can't think who else this person might be though. I don't know anyone else with a name that begins with a 'B'.

Looking back down at the letter, I read it again and realise that my hands are shaking. Whoever this guy is, Lily had for some reason only opened one of the letters and then hidden them all in here, away from Andy. I try not to let my imagination run too wild with all the possibilities of what this could mean.

There's a noise in the hallway and it makes me jump. My hands quickly thrust the envelopes back in the drawer and close it shut before picking up my swimming costume. I then leave the room. My legs are shaking as I walk down the hallway and pass Katrina, who is on her way to collect something from mother's room.

28th December 2020
12:10 pm

Ailish's car pulled up in the driveway at Balnair and she swung her long legs round from the driver's seat and got out. Opening the boot, she reached in for her gun and hunting bag. Lily came out from the house to meet her.

'Ailish! Great to see you. It's weeks since we last got together,' said Lily, leaning in for a hug. She noticed that Ailish looked a lot paler than usual, and her smile seemed false and forced. 'Is everything alright?' she asked.

'Aye. I'm fine. The blasted heater on this thing isn't working so I'm cold before we've even got going,' Ailish replied, pulling her hat firmly onto her head and taking out her gloves. 'Am I the first to arrive?'

Lily nodded.

'I haven't used my gun since I was at the range a few months ago, I could do with checking the Zero. Can I pop over to your range area quickly?' asked Ailish.

'Go ahead,' replied Lily. 'I think Andy and George are there now, doing the same thing with mine.'

Ailish disappeared around the side of the house and Lily frowned as she watched her go. Something didn't seem right with her. Moments later, the sound of a quad was heard as Broc drove into the driveway. His gun was strapped to the back of the four-wheel-drive machine.

Following behind him, on foot, was Will. He was wearing his biggest winter coat along with his hat and gloves. A pair of binoculars were hanging around his neck and he was carrying some ear defenders.

A shot was heard, firing from behind the house, and Will quickly put the ear defenders on and stood beside Lily.

'Och, come on Will. What's the point of coming with us if you're going to be like that all afternoon?' said Broc. His

61

voice sounded impatient, and he didn't smile as he spoke. Will stared at the ground, his face red with annoyance.

Broc walked over to Lily and looked at her hard for a moment.

'Are you okay Lily?' he asked. 'Everything alright?'

'Aye,' Lily smiled at him. 'Everything's fine, thank you.'

Broc looked at her for a bit longer and nodded before raising his eyes up towards the sky.

'A bit of cloud, but it'll be cold still. Make sure you wrap up.'

The sounds of more gunshots were heard, firing in quick succession and Will looked up, startled and nervous. Broc shook his head and turned away.

'I'll go and get my coat. Oh, and Andy's prepared a tray of single malts for everyone' said Lily, running back indoors.

When she returned outside, wearing her coat and carrying her hunting bag over her shoulder, the others had finished setting the rifles up and everyone was waiting in the driveway. Andy explained to them all where they were heading, and Lily passed the tray of drinks around. Broc shook his head. Lily frowned at him and offered the tray again. His face was stony, and his mouth set in a firm line. He met her concerned gaze and smiled a little, shaking his head again, insistent that he didn't want a drink. Lily put the tray down inside the doorway. Andy was still speaking.

'Sunset is at 3:38, so we'll probably stay up there until about 4pm. Maybe 4:15 at the latest, depending on the light. Lily has got a delicious stew in the slow cooker for us all to enjoy beside the firepit when we get back. Don't forget, its hind only; no stags. Stay in your seats unless you're going to follow up on a deer. If you do get down, radio it through so we all know where everyone is. Oh, and it's pretty cold too. Make sure you've got plenty of warm clothes with you. Any questions?'

He looked round at them all as they shook their heads. Broc seemed in some sort of mood and Ailish was obviously upset, she looked terrible. He'd need to speak to Ailish later, alone. Lily smiled at him and he smiled back. Laura had been right on the phone earlier; it wasn't quite like old times. Life threw curveballs sometimes.

'Alright then, let's go,' he said, pulling his brown hunting hat onto his head. 'It's quite a walk to the North Woods.'

Just Keep Swimming

It takes just a few seconds to walk the short distance from the house to the loch. On the other side of the bridge is an old track that leads down to a small, pebbly beach. The day is beautiful and if my thoughts weren't so distracted by the letter I've just read, I'd take a moment to stop and stare at the view. It's the sort of view that takes your breath away every time you see it. But not today. Today the wind has quite literally been taken out of my sails and there is nothing left for the view.

A young couple are setting up a small, two-man tent on the grassy area at the back of the beach. I cast them a brief, critical look.

Sadly, some of the wild campers who discover our loch are not very good at 'leaving no mark'. Over the years, we've had to pick up far too much disgusting litter and other waste which gets left behind by irresponsible people. These two appear to be okay though, and I hope they will leave everything neat and tidy when they move on.

I keep walking until I'm a good distance away from the campers and then take off my clothing and shoes. I'm already wearing my swimming costume underneath and so I quickly tiptoe my way across the pebbles to the shoreline. The sun is warm on my bare skin and the water is glistening in the sunlight. *'I love this loch so much,'* I think to myself and then edge my feet closer to the tiny rippling waves. As the icy-cold water touches my skin I let out a gasp and almost retreat, but I know the score. I've done this hundreds of times. Just a short shock of cold and then it will be alright.

I slowly inch my way into the loch and once the water reaches my belly button I pause for a moment, dropping my hands in and swishing them around in an attempt to acclimatise myself to the temperature. There's no point putting it off, I need to submerge now, or stand here like an idiot for the next fifteen minutes. I decisively allow my body to flop forwards into the water and then begin swimming about quickly. My head is up high, my strokes are short and messy, and my breaths are shallow and sharp. I'm sure that I must look anything but relaxed and comfortable.

After a minute or two though, I can feel my body beginning to relax. My breathing becomes steady and regular and, before long, I'm striking out in long, even strokes towards the middle of the loch.

This was actually a great idea. The exhilaration of swimming in my beloved loch is just what I need. With a wide smile, I kick hard and make my way through the water. Golden wagtails fly over, above my head, fish rise ahead of me and there is the distant sound of bleating sheep on the mountains. I can see the deep, dark water of the loch stretching away in front of me and I feel free.

Despite the fact that I've not been in a loch, or a lake or even a pool for a long time, I'm a strong swimmer. Growing up next to this insanely deep body of water, our father had ensured that both Andy and I could swim competently from an early age. Some summers it felt like we'd spent every day beside the loch, either swimming or kayaking up and down.

I still can't believe it has been twenty months since I was last here. Andy asked me last summer, over and over, when I was going to visit them. I'd kept putting off a trip home, still too consumed in my own bitterness. Instead, I'd assured him and Lily that I would return during the Christmas holidays to see them both, along with mother. But then the second wave of Covid had hit, and Boris Johnson and Nicola Sturgeon had told everyone that they couldn't travel and meet up, and so I'd never made it.

If I had been able to come home that week, I'd have been here that day when it all happened. I may even have been one of the suspects.

I swim all the way up towards a rocky outcrop where the side of the mountain drops directly into the water and then I stop. My arms feel tired and so I flip over onto my back and float for a while on the surface, gently pushing myself along with my legs.

The sky is a brilliant shade of piercing blue, with only a few wisps of cloud floating about like ribbons.

My thoughts go back to George. I'm thankful to have him here. Returning home yesterday to the house with no one there, except a mother who didn't know me and a medical employee, had not been the homecoming to which most young women aspire. The house feels different from how it used to be. It feels cold and empty, like it too is grieving over the tragedies that have occurred. Buddy is the only happy thing about it.

George is like family to me. He knows us all better than anyone else. He knows our secrets, and he keeps them.

George took care of everything for Andy's funeral. At first, I'd been concerned that, as a suspect, he wouldn't be able to do anything. But the police removed him from the inquiry very early on. There was no way it could have been him and so he was able to assist us with everything. There hadn't actually been a great deal to do. The funeral was delayed of course, due to the police investigation, but even so, when they eventually had released Andy's body, the country was still in lockdown and numbers were limited. As it was, there were only four of us present, in addition to the minister. That had been my decision. Mother didn't know what was happening, Lily was a complete wreck, and it was all still being covered daily in the papers. I wanted something quick and quiet, for all of us.

I stop kicking my legs and listen with my eyes closed. The sound of the lapping water is peaceful, restful.

Then the words of that letter appear against the darkness of my eyelids.

'I know he made you cry. He made you sad.'

Those words disturb me. It's not sitting right with me that Andy, the kindest, most caring guy ever, would make his own wife feel sad. Whoever this 'B' is, he's making a big accusation against my brother. Sorry, I mean, my late brother.

The words of that letter have again broken my peace and I realise that I'm beginning to feel cold, so I turn myself over and begin to swim back towards the beach. Getting out of the water, I quickly pick up my towel and begin to dry myself.

The couple I passed earlier now have their tent pitched and they are setting up a small stove to boil a kettle for some tea. They look happy and in-love. I envy them a little and find myself turning away so I don't have to watch them. Instead, as I struggle to pull my clothes back on and the denim of my shorts fights against my damp skin, I look up again at the loch and the view around me. Oxford may have become my sanctuary, but this place is truly a part of my soul.

In the distance, on the opposite side of the shore, a movement catches my attention. Someone is fishing. I guess that it's probably Will. I lift my hand to wave to him but know that he won't see me. He'll be fully engrossed in what he's doing, as always. I haven't even thought about Lily's family since I arrived yesterday. It would be rude if I don't call and see them.

As I make my way back to the house, I decide that later this evening, once I've eaten dinner, I'll take a walk up to the Mitchell's cottage and see how they're doing.

Police Interview Between Detective Chief Inspector Shaw (DCIS) and William Mitchell (WM)

DCIS: Mr Mitchell, you've told me that you don't like guns or shooting. If that is the case, then why did you go hunting with the others?

WM: Lily asked me to go.

DCIS: Did you want to go?

WM: I wanted to be with Lily.

DCIS: I see. So, you all went to the woods for the afternoon. The others all had their rifles and equipment. What did you do?

WM: I stayed with Andy and Lily.

DCIS: They were in a high seat, weren't they?

WM: Aye.

DCIS: Where were you?

WM: I waited at the bottom, on the ground.

DCIS: Why didn't you sit on the seat?

WM: There's not enough room for three people.

DCIS: When was the last time that you saw your brother-in-law?

WM: When he came down from the seat.

DCIS: I understand that your brother-in-law, Mr McClintock, went to see the others after a while.

WM: Aye.

DCIS: Did you go up on the seat with your sister then?

WM: No.

DCIS: You stayed at the bottom?

WM: Aye.

DCIS: Why didn't you sit with her?

WM: The guns are too loud.

DCIS: Ok. So, what did you do while you were waiting?

69

WM: I had my binoculars with me. I was looking for animals and birds.

DCIS: You told everyone that you saw Mr Henderson nearby to where you were, is that right?

WM: Aye.

DCIS: When did you see him?

WM: I don't know what time it was.

DCIS: Was it before or after any of the shots were fired?

WM: It was after the first shot but before the second one. I heard the second shot not long after I saw him.

DCIS: What was he doing?

WM: Walking up the woods.

DCIS: Did he have his rifle with him?

WM: Aye.

DCIS: Did you see him fire a shot at your brother-in-law?

WM: No.

DCIS: But you think that he did it, don't you?

WM: Aye.

DCIS: Mr Mitchell, can you explain to me why you think he did it?

WM: He looked angry. He had been angry all day. And he wasn't supposed to be there. He was supposed to be at his seat. I'm sure he did it.

DCIS: I'll ask you again, Mr Mitchell, did you see Brochan Henderson shoot Andrew McClintock?

WM: No.

DCIS: So, this is a guess then. You are guessing that he did it, are you? Mr Mitchell, can you answer the question? Is your accusation of Mr Henderson a guess?

WM: I think he did it.

DCIS: I see. Mr Mitchell, you said you don't like guns. Have you ever shot a rifle?

WM: No.

DCIS: Do you know how a rifle works? For the record... Mr Mitchell is shaking his head. Did you touch any of the rifles?

WM: No.

DCIS: Are you sure you didn't touch the rifles? Not even Mrs McClintock's rifle?

WM: No. I don't like rifles.

DCIS: Mr Mitchell, we have found your fingerprints on your sister's gun. I will ask you again. Did you touch it?

WM: Umm, I might have moved it.

DCIS: Why did you move it?

WM: I needed to move a few things. Everything was a mess. I might have moved her bag too.

DCIS: Did you touch anything else?

WM: No.

DCIS: Did you touch the ammunition?

WM: No. I just tidied things, that's all.

DCIS: I will repeat for the record that Mr Mitchell admits to the possibility of moving Mrs McClintock's rifle and bag. But denies touching the ammunition.

WM: I can't remember exactly. I just moved a few things.

DCIS: I have another question for you, Mr Mitchell. Did you like your brother-in-law?

WM: Aye.

DCIS: Was he nice to you?

WM: Aye, most of the time.

DCIS: What do you mean, 'most of the time?'

WM: Sometimes he was a bit impatient.

DCIS: Impatient about what?

WM: About me.

DCIS: Why was he impatient with you?

WM: I don't know. People are often impatient with me.

DCIS: Do you think that he and your sister were happy?

WM: Aye.

DCIS: Did anyone dislike your brother-in-law?

WM: No, I don't think so.

DCIS: Did Brochan Henderson like him?

WM: Aye.

DCIS: So, if Mr Henderson liked him, why do you think he shot him?

WM: Broc isn't very nice to people.

Visiting the Mitchells

With an early dinner digesting gently inside my stomach, I put my trainers on in order to walk over to the Mitchell's cottage. Holding the back door open, I whistle for Buddy and wait for him to run through it. In no time he's bounding ahead of me up the driveway, happy to be going out for a walk.

The sun is still fairly high in the sky and the air is still warm. The temperature feels unusual for this spot on the mountains, but I'm not about to complain. I follow the track which runs to the left of the loch and can't help but glance across the water to the beach. The young couple have lit a small fire on the shoreline and are cooking their evening meal. Everything is so peaceful.

Moving my attention away from them, I pick up a stick and throw it ahead, up the track and Buddy instantly runs off to retrieve it. Soon, he's returning as quickly as he can, carrying the slobbery thing in his mouth. He drops it at my feet for me to throw again. We walk in this way for about fifteen minutes. I assume that Buddy will get bored with the stick, but each time he brings it straight back and then drops it on the ground, barking excitedly and begging me to throw it again.

It's just under a mile to the other side of the loch where the Mitchell's cottage sits, nestled against the side of the mountain, hidden between trees. I can see that their cottage looks exactly the same as it always has. The white paint is still flaking off the window frames and the pointing between the bricks is still in desperate need of attention. As I approach, I wonder if the upkeep of the cottage is something that the Mitchells take care of or if it's actually the responsibility of the estate, and I make a mental note to ask George about it sometime.

The front door has been left ajar. I call out, 'Hello! Will? Mr Mitchell? Are you there?'

It's dark inside the narrow entranceway. Within a moment or two, I hear a movement from inside and then the sound of footsteps coming towards me. The shadow of someone comes into view and a voice calls back to me.

'Lil! you've come back!'

My heart sinks as I recognise Will's voice and the mistake he's just made. The sunlight behind me is bright. I realise that I must be silhouetted against the doorway, making it hard to see my face. He thinks it's Lily standing here.

'No. No, Will. It's me. It's Laura.' I quickly correct him and something inside twitches as I hear that name again, *'Lil'*.

Will steps closer and I can see him now. His smile is wide, despite his confusion at who I am. That twitch I felt a moment ago will have to wait for later though, as Mr Mitchell also now appears in the hallway. I notice though that, unlike Will, he is struggling to smile. His face is worn with the tell-tale lines of stress and worry.

'Ah Laura, dear, I'd heard you were back.'

I smile kindly at the man I've known my whole life.

'Yes,' I reply. 'I'm sorry that it's not under better circumstances.'

He nods. No words are needed to explain what I mean.

'You'll you have a drink with us?' he asks. 'It's a warm

evening, we can sit out here at the picnic table.'

I nod and walk over to the table to wait. Mr Mitchell heads back inside to get us all some lemonade whilst Will follows me. He's still smiling. He's clearly very happy to see me.

'How are you, Will?' I ask, watching as his fingers fiddle with the buttons on his shirt. He's always playing with something.

'I caught a couple of Brown Trout today and I saw a Haddy Char too. They're coming up soon. It's almost time for them to spawn,' he announces proudly.

The movements and numbers of the vulnerable Haddy Char are closely monitored at Balnair. This blue-grey fish with a yellowish belly is not often seen in many places but seems to have found a happy home in the quiet depths of our freshwater loch.

'That's good. I'm glad to hear that the Haddys are still around. What did you catch the trout on?' I ask. I've learned over the years what sort of questions to use when talking to Will.

He looks up at me, his face visibly excited that I've shown an interest in his hobby.

'One was on a Hare's Ear. The other was a Deer Caddis,' he replies. 'I tied them both myself.'

'Very good,' I say, pretending to understand what those two names even mean. 'I hope you threw them back if they were little.'

'Yes. Yes,' he says, looking down again at his shirt. 'I always do that.'

There is a moment of silence and then he looks up at me again.

'I missed you,' he tells me, reddening a little. 'You never

called me or even wrote to me.'

Will has always been bashful around girls and Lily often used to tease him when he wanted to hold my hand or sit close to me whilst we watched a film. As young children I'd allowed his attentions but as we got older, I'd tried not to encourage it too much.

'I'm sorry,' I reply, pulling an apologetic face. 'I've hardly called anyone since I left, and I didn't even think to write. I don't ever write to anyone.'

'We used to write to each other all the time,' he says.

I frown as, for a moment, I'm not sure what he means, but then I remember.

As children, the four of us would all write letters to one another. Each day, the postman would first stop at our house and then continue along the track and around the loch, to the Mitchell's place. We would often hand him a letter or two to deliver to Will and Lily, and they would send their replies back to us in the same way. I think it was by means of those letters that Andy and Lily, even as innocent little children, first developed feelings for each other.

'We haven't written letters to each other for years,' I say kindly.

Will opens his mouth to respond, but at that moment Mr Mitchell reappears with a tray of drinks.

I gratefully take a glass and sip from it.

'How's your mother?' asks Will's father.

'Her mind has deteriorated in the last twenty months, much worse than I imagined. I must say, it was a bit of a shock when I saw her last night.'

He lowers his glass to the table.

'It's scary what goes on in the human mind.'

There is an awkward silence and I know that we're both thinking of Lily.

'I'm going to contact the hospital in a day or two. Try to find out how long they think it will be before Lily can come back home,' I say.

'Lily hasn't spoken to either of us for about two months now. I'm not sure why.'

He looks so sad and I feel sorry for him.

Before I can say anything, Will spots a heron taking off from the edge of the loch and he begins talking, telling us some facts about the bird. Mr Mitchell and I both listen politely, grateful that the subject of the conversation has been changed.

We talk together for about thirty minutes, each of us avoiding the subject of that afternoon back in December. I have so many questions that I'm longing to ask, but as I watch Will talking about simple things such as the birds and the fish, I know that there is no point. His responses will provide no answers to my questions. After all, they had only left the police with more questions, so what good would they do me?

Will responds to people's questions in a way that tends to leave one with yet more things to ask. It's hard to get a full, complete picture from him. To be honest, I'm not yet mentally or emotionally ready to try and decipher Will's version of what he saw that day. Everything I've heard about that hunting trip so far has come from Inspector Shaw. I've heard it all third hand. I'm not entirely certain that I can cope with hearing the story being told from an eyewitness. That's why I've held back from questioning George too much. Yes, I've asked him about the money, and about how Lily was after everything happened, but as far as asking him about

77

what he saw...I'm not sure I'm ready to go there yet.

I finish my drink and then stand up to leave, explaining that I'm still tired from the journey.

'Can we see you again soon?' asks Will eagerly as I say goodbye to them both.

I look at him and a small twinge of envy comes over me. Here are his father and I, both grieving for the losses that life had dealt us, and yet Will seems to go on as normal. He's content with life's simple things and the most important question on his mind is that of when he will again see the girl next door. The girl he used to be sweet on.

'Probably,' I tell him, avoiding any commitment to anything. With a kind smile at them both, I whistle for Buddy and begin my walk back along the loch.

__What You Need to Understand about William__

William and Lilian Mitchell are twins, with Will being four minutes older than his sister. Their father, Alistair Mitchell, is the Balnair Gillie. He comes from a long line of gillies, running back three generations in the Mitchell family. Although Will loves fish and fishing more than anything else in the world, I don't think that he will be able to take on his father's role on the estate. You see, Will is on the autistic spectrum.

It's called a spectrum because the effects it has on those who are diagnosed varies greatly. Thankfully, Will can take care of himself physically. Well, I mean he can take care of the basic stuff, like washing and dressing etc. I'm not sure that, left alone for an entire week, he'd be able to cook, clean and look after himself to the necessary degree, but, in the main, he functions physically as any thirty-two-year-old guy would.

Where it's more obvious that Will suffers with autism is socially and mentally. He went to school with the rest of us in Inverness and, although he achieved some good grades in his exams, there's still something missing. He reminds of me a cog that's lost a few teeth; it still turns with the others, but nothing about it is smooth.

At school, Will was a whizz at things like algebra and equations, but then he couldn't work out simple, practical things. Like bank cards for example: Will never understood how they worked. If you gave him a purse full of money, he got it, but try to explain that you can pay for items in the supermarket with a small piece of plastic card and he can't understand it. It's something beyond him.

It's when you stop and talk to Will that you really realise something isn't right. He can make conversation well enough. He has a repertoire of questions that he will politely ask, but once you've replied, he doesn't then know what to say next. He never makes eye contact, and his body language is always a bit awkward. Talking to Will is hard work, unless you ask him something about fishing. Then his whole face will light up, a big smile will break out and he will talk for hours on his favourite subject.

Although Will was a part of our little gang, I wouldn't say that he was completely one of us. He was always there, tagging along, hanging on to either Lily or myself, but he was never truly involved in what was going on.

He would never understand our banter and dry ridicule of one another. An unusual array of activities tend to scare him or make him anxious and so he'd never be fully engaged in what we were doing.

Will and Broc clashed frequently. Will tends to gravitate towards people who are calm and kind. But Broc can be like a bull in a china shop with his words and has a habit of teasing people endlessly.

Since they were babies, William and Lilian Mitchell's names were shortened to Billy and Lily. It rolled nicely off the tongue.

Then, one day on the school bus, Broc decided to use that phrase we all know so well: 'Billy no mates'. In usual 'Broc style', he could see that it was creating a reaction and so he kept saying it, all that week and the next. It upset Will more than I think Broc realised. Will had a bit of a problem with his temper at times and eventually, when he'd had enough of the name calling, he picked up a rock and threw it at Broc in retaliation. Thankfully, it hit Broc's shoulder and not his head, but it could have been quite serious.

Since then, William insisted that we all call him 'Will' and would get really upset if we used the name 'Billy'. I think he's always had a jaded view of Broc since that day. That's something the autism seems to accentuate in him; he holds on to grievances and grudges, even over silly little things.

For all his awkwardness and funny, autistic ways, Will is a very loyal, caring guy. He adores Lily and he was fond of Andy. I think he liked the way that Andy would always try to include him in things, and would rarely get impatient with him either. For some reason, I too seemed to have found a special place in Will's heart over the years. When I was younger it used to annoy me a bit, the way he would follow me around like a puppy dog, but as I got older, I didn't mind. Lily was always so good with him, and I tried to be like her as much as I could.

As a kid, I soon learned that if you were in Will's good books, then it could work out to be advantageous.

I remember one occasion when Andy and I had been playing at the Mitchell's house. I think I was about eight years old and the others were ten, or thereabouts. Lily and Will's (or Billy, as he was still called back then) mother had made us a delicious chocolate cake. We'd each been given a slice and then she'd carefully put the last piece away in the cupboard for Mr Mitchell to have when he returned from work.

I'd enjoyed the cake so much that I just couldn't resist

it. Whilst the others were in the living room, playing with a pack of 'Happy Families', I'd sneaked back into the kitchen and eaten the last piece of cake.

I knew it was wrong and I really shouldn't have done it, but it tasted so good. I can remember, licking the sweet, butter-icing off my fingers and then closing the cupboard door as quietly as I could. I turned around and went back to the living room where I continued playing with the others, thinking that I'd got away with the whole thing.

About thirty minutes later we heard a shout of rage from the kitchen and all of our heads shot up, anxiously. As Mrs Mitchell called for each of us to get in there at once, Will caught hold of my arm and used his own sleeve to wipe the side of my mouth. Wide eyed, I'd looked at him, realising that he was wiping the remnants of chocolate from my lips.

Once we were all in the kitchen, Mrs Mitchell held the empty plate out in front of us and demanded to know who was responsible. I remember my legs shaking as I realised the trouble that I was now going to be in. Andy and Lily both shrugged and said that it wasn't them. With my lip beginning to wobble, I was about to own up to it all when Will stepped forwards and pointed at Lily.

'No!' he said defiantly. 'It was Lily.'

'It wasn't me!' protested Lily. 'I'd never steal cake from father.'

'It must have been you,' continued Will. 'When you went to get the cards, you took it. I bet that's what you did.'

Lily then started to cry, and I still feel bad that I didn't speak up and admit that it was me, but something about the relief of not being told off stopped me from doing so.

Later, I whispered to Will, 'Why did you say it was Lily?'

'Because I like you,' he replied. 'Besides, Lily upset me yesterday and I wanted to get her back.'

That's our Will. He doesn't quite understand the social etiquettes. He tends to be ruled by his current emotions. And yet, he is really very sweet and fiercely loyal to those he loves. Despite his funny ways, we're all fond of him.

Will and Lily's mother died about a year after the incident with the cake. She had cancer. Since then, Lily became like a mother to her brother and looked after him as any loving sister would. That's how he became part of our group really. I don't think he'd have spent so much time with us all if Lily hadn't felt the need to keep an eye on him so much.

The loss of Andy, the situation Lily is now in, and the breakdown of our little friendship group is something I've been really struggling with. I expected Will to be struggling too, but I guess I've forgotten that he's not like the rest of us. Emotions don't quite affect Will the same as they do others. I've forgotten that he tends to live in the moment, unless of course he is holding a grudge against something, and then he's stuck in the past for a period of time until he gets over it. That's why he was content to just talk about fishing, while his father was clearly still battling the events that life had thrown at him. But I have no doubt that underneath his veil of autism, Will must be struggling in his own way, as I'm sure the others are too.

28th December 2020
1.45 pm

They all arrived at the lower slope of the North Woods and Andy stopped beside the first high seat. He swung his bag to the ground.

'Lily and I will take this seat. Will, you can stay here with us. George, can you continue up with Broc and Ailish? You can leave Ailish at the next seat, it's not far from here, and then maybe you and Broc can take the other two at the top of the woods. Perhaps if you take the furthest one that's just by the clearing?'

George nodded. 'Has everyone got their radios?'

They all took them out.

'Channel three,' confirmed George, and they all tested them. 'Nobody moves without radio contact first. Am I clear?' He gave Will a meaningful look and they all nodded in response.

Andy spoke again. 'I'll probably sit with Lily for about an hour and then I'll come up to each of you towards the end of the afternoon. I'll be stalking from behind. I'm not really here for the deer today. I'm here for you guys,' He grinned at them all. Broc still looked moody, and Andy frowned. He'd find out later what was up with him.

'Right, we'll leave you three here then,' said George, leading the way off through the woods.

'Up you go, Lily,' said Andy, holding her rifle for her. 'I'll pass everything up to you once you're settled.'

Will took a blanket out of his rucksack and laid it on the floor. He sat down and put his ear defenders on.

'Remember, Will, you mustn't move from that spot.'

Will nodded and rolled his eyes. He felt like the others treated him like a baby sometimes.

'I mean it. I don't care if you get scared. You don't move at all!' Andy knew his voice was firm, but Will had a tendency to sometimes ignore instructions and he couldn't afford any risks. Safety was of the utmost importance.

Andy climbed up and sat next to Lily. She had already set her rifle up, balancing it against the ledge at the front of the seat, and was now taking out her thermal imager and binoculars. Andy smiled to himself. She'd only applied for her licence and begun shooting at the start of the pandemic, but she was already very competent. She'd been so shaky and nervous when they'd first started out with target practices about eight months ago, but now she was proficient. He liked watching her shoot. Lily lacked a lot of confidence in most things. Her head often got the better of her in tests of mental endurance, so it brought him joy to watch her take control of something.

Andy had wondered at first if his wife might be too delicate to cope with taking a kill, but she'd surprised him and shown herself to be a much stronger woman than he'd imagined. He'd soon discovered that she was a natural hunter.

Lily shot her first deer, an adult red stag, about four months ago. Andy wasn't sure at the time if it had been a bit too much and broken her. As the magnificent animal dropped to the floor, instantly killed by her clean, precise shot, she'd shaken uncontrollably and begun to cry. He'd worried for a moment whether he'd possibly pushed her too far, but after a few minutes she'd pulled herself together and they'd gone over to check it. To his delight, Lily had been fine. She'd even enjoyed skinning it and butchering it, once they'd managed to get it home.

'Have you got everything you need?' he asked her, keeping his voice low.

'Aye, I just need to load the magazine and then I'm ready,' she replied, putting her hand on the bolt handle and sliding it back. She'd taken her gloves off to load the mag and the metal felt cold against her fingers. Once she'd placed it inside and slid the bolt forward, she double checked the safety was on and then turned her attention to the woodland ahead.

The north woodland area was hard for shooting. It was a large area, made up of mostly coniferous trees, which had been planted decades ago following a decline of the Scottish woodland at the end of the nineteenth century. Unlike some of the smaller deciduous areas on the estate, the amount of foliage on the trees at this time of year meant that it was harder to spot the deer as they moved about. The high seats were all positioned close to trails and tracks that were regularly used by the deer, but that still didn't make it any easier. It was Lily's least favourite area on the estate to hunt, but it was the largest area where they could all sit in one place and not have to stalk on the move. So, for today's activities, it was the perfect choice.

Lily and Andy sat in silence for about thirty minutes. Each time she saw a movement she reached for her binoculars, only to confirm that it was just a weasel or even a squirrel disturbing the branches.

'Where are all your reds, Andy?' asked Broc over the radio. 'Only birds and weasels where I'm sitting.'

Andy reached into their bag for a radio. 'I blame Lily, she's had a great start to the late season,' he replied.

'It's pretty cold waiting for nothing,' chirped in Ailish.

'Remind me again, why exactly we're all sitting still like this and not stalking?' asked Broc, his voice audibly gruff with annoyance.

'You know why,' replied Andy, refusing to be drawn into a conversation that might make William feel unwanted.

Andy sighed contently as the radios went silent and Lily kept on watching the woods. After a while she put the binoculars to one side and looked at Andy. He was sitting on the step just below her, deep in his own thoughts.

'Don't worry about Broc's comments,' she said. 'Will wouldn't have understood their meaning anyway.'

'It's not that,' he answered. 'Although, I'll admit, I feel a bit like Broc. A stalk would have been a much better idea.'

'Well, I'm grateful that you've included Will, even if Broc isn't,' Lily whispered, squeezing his arm gently.

Andy smiled and then looked away again. His thoughts were clearly a million miles away from where they were both sitting.

'Are you missing Laura?' she asked softly.

He nodded. 'She's never missed the end-of-year deer hunt before.'

'She'd have been here, if it wasn't for the pandemic. You know that.'

'Aye, I know.' He fell silent again.

'Did it seem to you like something is wrong with Broc?' Lily asked, after a few moments had passed.

Andy looked up at her. 'Aye. I'm going to pop over to his seat in a bit and see what's going on.'

'I haven't seen him look moody or sulky for a long time.'

'No,' agreed Andy. 'Something's clearly bothering him.'

'And Ailish too,' added Lily. 'She loves hunting and yet she looked sad when she arrived, as though she'd been crying. Did she say anything to you while you were zeroing the guns?'

Lily noticed that Andy shifted his weight uncomfortably as he replied, 'No, she didn't say anything.'

Lily was about to ask if he knew of any reason that Ailish might be upset but she stopped herself. Years ago, she'd been wary of Ailish, and she'd questioned her every move. She'd always felt that Ailish didn't like her much and it was widely known by everyone that Ailish had desperately traipsed around after Andy when they were all younger. For a few years, Lily had struggled to completely trust the motives of the other woman, especially after her and Andy had finally got together. Ailish had seemed to be clingy with Andy initially, as if she was trying to prove something and Lily had felt jealous for a while, but she'd worked hard on her feelings and overcome them. She knew that old Mr McClintock and Mr Briars' family went back a long way as friends. In the end, Lily realised that Andy had chosen her and married her, not Ailish, and so she'd learned not to worry about things.

Reflecting on Everything

An intense feeling of sadness washes over me as I make my way back home from the Mitchell's cottage. The sun has dropped behind the mountains and is casting long shadows across the loch. I shiver to myself. Untying the arms of my jumper from around my waist, I pull it over my head and smooth the warm fleecy material down across my body.

I realise that I feel very alone.

My mother, who I had at one stage begun to view as a true friend and not just an authoritarian, matronly figure in my life, no longer knows who I am. My father, who had adored me and spoiled me completely, has been dead and buried for over three years. And then there's Andy, the brother I had looked up to in everything. He's also now gone, having been cruelly taken away from me long before his time.

And of course, there are my friends... Lily, my sweet, delicate, sister-in-law, is now lost to a world of mental anxiety and anguish. Ailish, who I would normally have turned to first at a time like this, is still 'a person of interest' and that stands between us both now like a huge hurdle that I can't seem to see over, let alone start to tackle. And then there's Broc, and, well, I don't even want to think about him anymore.

There are so many things I feel I need to talk through with someone, issues that require attention, questions that need answering, but I have no one to turn to for help and advice. I can feel my eyes pricking as tears threaten to escape, but I manage to hold them back. I'm not one for crying. Don't get me wrong, I'm emotional. Sometimes my body shakes as I struggle to control the feelings inside of me. Or my stomach churns over, threatening to bring up its contents. Occasionally, I even get that burning sensation against my eyes, as tears threaten to fall. But, in my opinion, only silly girls cry and I'm not a silly girl.

In the last few years, I've only cried a handful of times. Tears obviously poured from my eyes around the time of Andy's death and at his funeral. Before that, the last time I cried was when I left Balnair and I found out that... never mind. I don't need to tell you about that.

I attempt to focus my thoughts on some of the decisions I will shortly need to make. The first of those, and it is actually the most important, is what I'm going to do with the estate.

Andy inherited the McClintock land and became Laird of Balnair after father's death. At the time I was insanely jealous. My heart and soul used to belong to this place, beside this loch. The thought that it all belonged to my brother, and would never belong to me, drove me wild. It seemed so unjust, that he should get something I loved so much, just because he was male.

I think I stopped talking to him for about a fortnight. It upset him greatly, of course: my unreasonable behaviour. And that's exactly what it was; unreasonable. Andy was the kindest, most conscientious person in the world. He knew I loved this place with a great passion, and he told me that it would always be my home, no matter who was the owner on paper. I came around in the end, but I was stubbornly long in doing so.

Then everything changed, and I suddenly wanted to be as far away from the Highlands and from Balnair as possible. I moved to Oxford, set up a new, happy little life there and swore I'd never move back.

The problem is that Balnair is now mine. I am now the laird (or perhaps I should say, the lady). I've longed for this place to be mine all my life and now that it finally is, I'm not sure that I want it anymore.

What's the point in owning a place as beautiful as this, if you've got no one to share it with?

I now walk along, picking at bits of grass and pulling leaves apart and think of Andy. I still can't believe that he's been murdered. Those words have still not sunk in, even eight months later. No one hated Andy. He was the guy that everyone loved. Everyone wanted to be friends with Andy. To me, the idea of someone having a motive to want him dead is ridiculous. And yet Inspector Shaw still believes that someone might actually have had reason to do it. That's why the investigation is still ongoing, even though no one has been charged.

My mind again goes back to that letter which was addressed to Lily. The one that's laying in the bottom of my chest of drawers. And then something twitches again, as it had when I was talking to Will.

Will had mentioned the letters we used to write to each other when we were kids.

I stop walking and put my hands on my hips. As I stare up at the sky, I realise that I know who the mysterious 'B' is.

It's Will, signing his name as 'B' for 'Billy': the name we'd used when he was a little boy. He wrote that letter to Lily. He wished that she'd never moved out and wanted her to go home.

He'd even mistaken me for Lily and called me 'Lil' when I arrived at the house. It must be something he'd called Lily when they'd been growing up, although it wasn't a name that I'd ever heard him use around others.

A small wave of relief washes over me as I realise that the letter is from Will. For a moment I'd been worried that Lily had been having some sort of affair behind Andy's back.

But my relief is short lived.

I soon remember the contents of the letter and I feel my throat constrict a little as I come to the realisation that, for some reason, Will thought that Andy had been making Lily sad.

But surely Will must have been mistaken, I reason. I've known Will for years and many times he's been overly sensitive and emotional about something that turned out to be small and inconsequential. That must be what had happened. He must have taken something he'd seen or heard the wrong way and come to the wrong conclusions about it all. That must be it, surely.

But if Will had come to that conclusion, would that have given him a reason to dislike, even to hate, Andy? Would that have given him motive for murder?

My legs begin shaking as I take in the prospect and the implications of that possibility.

I'm almost at the house and my anxious thoughts are interrupted as my phone connects with the Wi-Fi from the building and the sound of WhatsApp notifications ping from my pocket.

Amongst the messages are two from Cassie, an old school friend who lives in Inverness.

The first begins with an emoji of a spy, followed by the words, *'I hear you're back!'*

There are no prizes for guessing how the news of my return to Scotland has travelled so quickly. Cassie's grandmother lives in Foyers and is a friend of the gossiping Mrs Tweedle.

The second message is an invitation to meet her for lunch.

I think about it for a moment. My natural instinct is to say no, but I pause before replying. I've just been feeling lonely and here is an old friend reaching out to me. Cassie is sweet. She'd never try to meet up with me just to feed her curiosity, which is something I'm aware that others would do. She's a genuine girl. We used to get on well when we went to school together, and we've often met up over the years. Besides, I need to go to Inverness and do a big food shop anyway so, why not meet up with her at the same time?

'That would be lovely. Lunch? Tomorrow?' I reply, before pocketing my phone and going inside to see mother.

Meeting the Postie

For the second night running, I sleep well and awake to another bright, sunny day. I roll over and look at the time; 8:30am. Wow! Whatever it is about the Highland air, it's curing my eight-month long bout of insomnia.

With an hour or two to kill before I need to leave for Inverness, I unpack my laptop and carry it down to the small study which is positioned just off the hallway. Everything in the room is an untidy jumble of paperwork and I sigh as I push it all to one side in order to make room for my laptop. At some point over the next few days, I'll need to organise the mess in this room, but I can't face it today. Instead, I open the lid to my laptop, turn it on and go to check my emails.

Apart from a reminder to order new contact lenses and a promotion from Groupon, the inbox is empty. Feeling disappointed, I close the lid.

My boss is being true to his word. Despite my arguments, he'd insisted that for two weeks, all my work would be looked after by others in the office and my emails were to be forwarded to my colleagues.

'Take this time as compassionate leave,' he'd told me kindly. 'Laura, if anyone needs it, it's you. Give yourself two weeks to work out what the situation is back home and then we can work something out, remotely or otherwise.'

I should really be grateful for his kindness, but I would have preferred it if they hadn't diverted all my emails. The non-emotionally charged exercise of completing work tasks is something I feel I need to do in order to cope with the reality of what I'm facing.

I end up spending the next ninety minutes mindlessly scrolling through Instagram posts on my phone before deciding it's time to shower and get dressed.

By 11:00am, I'm ready to go, having washed and dried my hair. Wearing a simple summer dress, I make my way out to the car and instinctively climb again into the front seat of Eileen. As I'm about to pull the door shut, I hear the sound of tyres on gravel and look up to see the post van pull into the yard.

Buddy comes bounding round the corner, his tail wagging furiously as a guy, about the same age as me, gets out from the driver's seat of the van. He's got mousy-coloured, curly hair and a lop-sided grin.

'Hey Buddy,' he calls and kneels down, taking a small biscuit from his pocket. I watch as he holds his hand out towards my dog. Buddy seems to know exactly what is expected of him and immediately offers the guy his paw with his tongue hanging hungrily out of his mouth. The postman gives Buddy the much longed for biscuit and then reaches back inside the van for a small bundle of envelopes.

'I see Buddy has made a new friend in my absence,' I say, getting out the car and smiling at the stranger.

He looks up, slightly startled. 'Oh, I'm sorry, I didn't see you there,' he replies and comes over, carrying the post.

'I'm Laura. Laura McClintock,' I say, awkwardly holding my hands by my side as I'm afraid of all the 'Covid carrying' letters he must touch throughout the day.

'Ah.' His face turns solemn. 'I'm very sorry about your brother. He was such a nice guy.'

'Yes, he was,' I answer, unsure of what else I should say.

'Would you like to take the post, or shall I give it to Mr Thompson?'

'I'm just on my way out, so if you could give it to George, that would be great,' I say, getting back into the Land Rover.

I put the key in the ignition and then pause before turning it. It occurs to me that at least one thing could be set straight in my head today.

'I'm sorry, I didn't ask your name,' I call out after the friendly postman who is now heading towards the door to George's office.

He turns around.

'It's Angus,' he calls back.

I wait for Angus to give the post to George and make his way back towards me.

'Angus, would you mind clearing something up for me?' He looks at me blankly and I continue talking, 'I found a small bundle of unaddressed letters yesterday while I was searching around in a chest of drawers.'

Angus frowns. He's clearly confused.

I decide to cut to the chase. 'Over the past few months, did William, Lily's brother in the cottage on the other side of the loch, give you any letters for her?'

A look of recognition comes over his face.

'Aye, you're right, he did. He hasn't sent any for a while now though. I was a bit confused at the time, but I'm glad to know they got to where they were meant to. It didn't quite make sense to me, but George seemed to understand and said he'd pass them onto to Mrs Lily as she'd know what to do with them.'

I smile. I had been correct with my guess. Will is the writer of the letters to Lily.

'It's an old tradition,' I explain. 'Mr Hancock, the previous postman, used to deliver our private letters to each other when we were all young. Will must have thought you'd understand it all.'

Angus nods.

'Mr Hancock's boots have been hard to fill,' he says, shrugging slightly. 'He was a very popular man.'

'Well, you seem to be gaining a popularity of your own,' I grin, looking down at Buddy who is sitting calmly and staring intently at Angus.

'Aye,' he laughs. 'If I can make friends with the pets, then the owners are like putty in my hands.'

I'm about to say goodbye when something else occurs to me.

'Do you always give the post to Mr Thompson?' I ask.

'Aye,' he nods. 'Mr Andrew was normally out somewhere on the estate and Mrs Lily, well, I only met her a few times. Then, after, well, after it all...' He coughs nervously. 'Anyway, I just take it directly to Mr Thompson now.'

I smile warmly. 'It was nice to meet you, Angus.'

Closing the car door, I start the engine. Angus gets back into his van, turns it around and I follow him out of the driveway. He gives a cheery little beep on the horn as he continues along the loch and down the track to the Mitchell's place while I turn right and cross the bridge. As the road winds round, away from the house, I pause for a moment on the bend and look out, down at the view. The water is shimmering in the sunlight, the air is still and the reflections of the mountains on either side are perfect. I really do love this place. The two campers, who spent the night sleeping on the shore of Balnair, are now packing their tent away into their huge backpacks, preparing to move on. I hope they've enjoyed their stay beside my beautiful loch.

Along the side of the loch, I can see Angus' van, still making its way steadily along the track. I'm glad I met him today. He's confirmed the conclusion I made last night about the writer of that letter. That's one less thing to bother me.

Feeling more settled than I did yesterday, I pull my sunglasses out from my bag and put them on. After winding both windows down, I put Eileen in gear, and make my way to Inverness.

28th December 2020
2:45pm

'If you don't mind, I'll walk up and check on the others,' said Andy.

Lily nodded.

Andy held his radio in front of his mouth. 'Ailish. I'm coming over to you, I'll approach from behind. Over.'

Silence.

Andy repeated himself.

There was a faint crackle of something, as if someone was responding.

'I'll go to Ailish first,' he said, starting to climb down from the seat. 'I can approach her safely from behind. It sounds like she heard me and we're just getting some interference in her reply.'

Will was still sitting at the bottom of the seat, leaning back against a tree. He looked cold and miserable.

'You can sit up with Lily if you want,' offered Andy.

Will shook his head. He didn't like heights as well as loud noises.

Andy shrugged to himself. He tried not to be annoyed. They'd deliberately not gone on a stalk so that Lily's brother could safely come with them, but what was the point of him coming, if he was just going to sit on the floor alone all afternoon? Will's face went red. He sensed that Andy was frustrated with him. He remembered a time when Andy never used to get annoyed. Andy was always kind and calm, but recently he'd been impatient with him. Will didn't know what he'd done wrong. He'd heard Andy and Lily talking together, up in the seat. He heard Andy say he was missing Laura. Will missed her too. She was always kind and patient with him, even when the others weren't. He wished she'd come home for the holidays. He felt lonely without her.

Andy walked off towards the next seat. His steps were slow and deliberate. He didn't want to startle any deer that might be nearby.

After a few minutes he approached Ailish's seat.

'Hey,' he whispered and climbed up towards her.

She jumped.

'What are you doing?! Why didn't you radio to say you'd left your seat?' she hissed.

'I did. I thought I heard you talking back, but it was all crackly,' he replied.

'Well, I didn't hear anything. Your radio must have stopped working.'

'Are you alright?' he asked, looking up at her.

'I'm blinking freezing!' she snapped back.

'No, you know what I mean.'

'Aye. Although I'm so tired all the time. I just hate this whole situation,' she smiled weakly. 'Thanks for being here for me though. I really don't know what I'd do without you.'

'Lily was asking if everything is okay. She can tell something isn't right.'

Ailish bit her lip. 'What did you tell her?'

'Nothing,' he replied. 'I told her I didn't know what was wrong.' He paused. 'I lied to her,' he added bitterly.

Ailish didn't reply.

'She'll find out at some point,' continued Andy. 'I'd rather be able to say something myself. I'd like to explain what I've been doing, before she works it all out for herself or, worse still, someone else works it out. I don't like to keep secrets from Lily.'

'I know,' replied Ailish. 'Can you just give me a few more weeks? Let things settle a bit my end?'

Andy let out a sigh. 'Okay, but I want to let her know what's been going on soon. Alright?'

Ailish nodded.

Andy smiled, 'I'm going to go up to Broc, can I use your radio, if you don't think mine is working?'

She passed him her radio and he spoke into it.

'Broc, It's Andy, I'm coming up to you. I'll take a direct route from seat two. Over.'

'Got that. I'll look out for you,' replied Broc's voice. It sounded hard and moody.

Andy passed the radio back to Ailish and reached up to take hold of her hand. He squeezed it gently.

'Everything will be alright,' he said, and she gave him a watery smile.

Into Inverness

It takes me almost an hour to get to Inverness. It's a journey we used to take day after day on the school bus.

Some days the time would fly by as we'd all be laughing and joking together. Other times it would drag. There might have been an argument or even a fight between someone and the whole atmosphere would be tense. The trip to school each day dragged loads during my last year. That was after Andy, Broc, Will and Lily had all finished their education, and it was just me, mostly sitting there alone, wishing that Ailish lived outside the city with us so that we could travel to and from school together.

With still another two weeks left of the holidays, I've anticipated that it might be busy in the city centre and so drive directly to a quiet road called Glenburn Drive. I left home early in order to leave time for the small walk along the river to where I'm meeting Cassie. It allows me to stretch my legs as well as avoiding the expensive fees in the city carparks. Having bumped Eileen up onto the kerb and parked her against a hedge, I now make my way towards the bank of the river Ness.

Although it's fairly busy along the footpath, it's actually quieter than I expected it would be and the short walk into the centre is pleasant. I can see why the tourists come here. It has a charm you don't find elsewhere.

I arrive at the Castle Tavern. It's a pub which sits on the junction of three roads with a small triangular courtyard at the front. Cassie is already there waiting for me, having successfully grabbed an empty table in the sun. She looks up as I open the gate and smiles, waving happily at me. As I approach, she gets up from her seat and opens her arms, 'Are we hugging, or not hugging?'

I hesitate for a moment as my Covid anxiety threatens to take over, but then I make a decision. 'Hugging,' I reply and reach out to give her a warm embrace.

Pulling back, Cassie looks at me for a moment, analysing my appearance.

'Laura, I love this new look!' she says.

I raise my eyebrows in response.

'Seriously!' she insists. 'You look like you've lost a couple of pounds, not that you even needed to, but it makes your waist look amazing. And then there's your hair! I never understood why you used to dye it. Your natural colour is so beautiful! And with it grown out a bit...you look like Nicole Kidman, when she was younger of course!'

I laugh. Cassie is sweet. She's always been one to praise and compliment people, but I'm definitely no Nicole Kidman. And, as for the reason I used to dye my hair... well, that reason ended when I left Scotland, so it doesn't seem to matter anymore whether it's my natural colour or not.

We sit down and a waiter quickly arrives at our side and hands us two menus.

'When did you get back?' Cassie asks. Her questions are genuine, no hint of prying for information.

'Only two days ago,' I reply. 'But you know how it is in a place like Foyers, news travels faster than a pigeon can carry it. Especially anything that involves the

McClintocks, hey?'

Cassie smiles kindly. 'Especially if it involves people like Mrs Tweedle.'

The waiter returns and takes our order. I decide to go for the Cullen Skink. I haven't eaten it for so long and I remember that they cook it well here.

'So, how is everything in Oxford? You sound more English than ever before!'

I shake my head and try not to laugh. Cassie is attempting to speak with an English accent, but it sounds more like a bad attempt at Welsh. It's true though. My accent has always been a very soft version of Scottish, despite being born and raised in the Highlands. Our father was a Scot, through and through, but he'd married an English girl and I think that living at home with my mother influenced the way my own accent developed over the years. I don't even use a lot of Scottish expressions when I'm talking. Sometimes I sound like an outsider.

'You know, everyone in England thinks my accent is very Scottish,' I reply, with mock indignation. 'They don't understand half of what I say.'

'Never!' she laughs. 'That's impossible. You don't sound Scottish at all. I blame your mother,' says Cassie and then frowns to herself. 'I'm sorry. Your poor mother. How is she?'

'She's not good,' I admit. 'I'm pretty sure she has no idea who I am.'

'It's sad, isn't it?'

I nod and glance over the road at the castle. From here it has the appearance of something more like a stately home, but I know that the red, sandstone building stretches back behind the front that I can see. Just around the corner, hidden from our view, is an impressive structure of towers and turrets.

'So, Oxford... What is your place like?' Cassie kindly changes the subject.

I think about my cosy little flat, next to the river, overlooking one of the famous colleges.

'It's a lovely city,' I tell her. 'Very similar to here really. The river Thames flows through the city. It's popular for punting.'

'What on earth is punting?'

I ponder about how best to describe it.

'It's a sort of long shallow boat,' I try to explain. 'You can seat about half a dozen people in it. You don't row it though. One of you stands at the back with a long pole and uses it to push the boat through the water. It's a bit like the boats you see in photos of Venice.'

'Ah, okay. So does a driver come with you or do you drive it yourself?' she asks.

'No, you drive it yourself. I think that's why it's so popular. It's actually chaos, if I'm honest,' I add, thinking back to a team-building day at work when we'd all gone punting and I'd almost fallen off the back of the punt as I got the pole stuck firmly in the riverbed.

'And is your work going well?' Cassie is so good at showing interest in people.

'Yes, it is,' I reply. 'It was hard at first because we went into lockdown just a few weeks after I started there. I could still work remotely, but I didn't get to know the others well at all. But then last summer, once we were allowed back into the office, it was better. It's a really nice team of people.'

Cassie smiles. 'Now, the biggest question I've been waiting to ask, and I think it's probably the most exciting one too, is...'

I hold my breath, bracing myself for her inevitable question about Andy.

She continues, 'Have you met Inspector Morse yet?'

I breathe a quiet exhalation of relief and smile in response to her.

It's funny how everyone seems to ask me that question. I've never seen an episode of 'Morse' and so I have no idea what the obsession with it is.

'No,' I tell her, solemnly. 'I've not met him. But to be honest, I've had more than my fair share of contact with detective inspectors over the past few months.'

Cassie's face pales a little and I realise that she's been deliberately avoiding the subject of Andy and his death.

'I'm really sorry about everything, Laura,' she says, and I can sense the relief in her voice that I've mentioned it first. 'It must have been pretty awful for you.'

'I was glad to be away when it happened, if I'm honest,' I say, picking at my napkin.

'I can only imagine.' I can feel Cassie's eyes watching me carefully as she's clearly unsure of how much to say on the subject. 'It was all over the papers for a while and people were talking a lot.'

'As they would,' I shrug. 'It's only natural, I suppose.'

There's a pause for a moment. I can tell that Cassie is contemplating her next words.

'I don't suppose you've bumped into 'Prince Charming' yet have you?'

I look up to meet her eyes and feel the colour drain from

my own face.

The History of Me and Broc

I think of Broc and feel a weird, fluttering sensation inside. It's a mixture of sadness and joy.

I'd loved Brochan Henderson for as long as I could remember. His family's farm borders the Balnair estate and that made us neighbours my whole life.

I've often asked myself why I loved him as much as I did and I'm never quite sure how to answer.

Broc isn't what most women would call 'handsome'. His looks are far from that of your traditional 'Prince Charming'. He looks more like a medieval knight with his rugged features and large torso. And there's nothing very charming about his personality either. In fact, Broc has a wicked, dry sense of humour and a tendency to look down on others. That was why some of the girls at school had nicknamed him 'Prince Charming'. It was a name they used in jest as they'd found him to be very much the opposite. Broc's overall manner is a bit proud, and he is shallow too. There had always been a girl or two trailing around though, enamoured by his overbearing masculinity, but he would always turn down the plain girls, preferring the ones with prettier faces instead.

Broc was Andy's best friend and I'd often thought of them as Mr Bingley and Mr Darcy, from Jane Austen's 'Pride and Prejudice', when they were together. Like Bingley, Andy was kind, open and loved by everyone. And then there was Broc: a true Mr Darcy. He was proud and arrogant. He was a closed book.

No, I wasn't really sure why I'd loved him. Perhaps it

was because he captured the essence of Scotland and our Highland life. It was a life I loved growing up and he was a rugged part of it.

I always believed that Broc and I would end up together, as a happily married couple.

But then he met that girl from Edinburgh: Jessica.

They met while he was away on Andy's stag do. She had apparently been part of a hen group that was also karting that day. Jessica was tall, blonde, and beautiful. I assumed that she'd come and go, as every girlfriend he'd ever had before had done. But she didn't. She stayed. It was a whirlwind romance of just a few months and then one day they announced their engagement. That was the moment when I knew that it was I who had to go. I couldn't stay here on the estate with Broc next door, married to some trophy wife.

Finding out about Broc's engagement and then making the decision to move away was one of the few things in recent years that caused me to cry. I remember that I'd gone and stood out by the loch and cried big, wet tears to myself. Shamefully, Will had appeared and seen me. He was awkward, as always, and I'd quickly wiped my cheeks dry, embarrassed to have been caught in a moment of, what I felt to be, girly weakness.

I can remember the day when I told Broc that I wouldn't be attending the wedding. It was December 2019, just four weeks before his and Jessica's big day.

'Why ever not, Wee Ginge?' he'd asked, confirming that he had no idea of my feelings towards him. 'You have to be there! You're one of my best friends.'

With that sentence, I knew that I was making the right decision. The estate was now Andy's. He and Lily had married just ten months earlier. I had no reason to stay.

It was time for me to find my own way in life. Especially now I'd been eternally put in Broc's 'friend zone'.

'I've found a job,' I'd shrugged, trying to hide the bitter disappointment that I felt inside. 'I start on January 2nd.'

'But you can still travel back for my wedding, surely!'

I remember that he'd looked sad. Hurt a little even. I'd then moved my eyes away from his and looked at something in the distance.

'The job's in Oxford.'

'Oxford,' he'd exclaimed. 'Whatever are you moving to Oxford for?'

'Because then I'll never have to bump into you and your perfect wife,' I thought to myself before replying, 'Well, there's nothing to stay around here for, and it's a great opportunity.'

The second part was a lie. The job was simple. A legal secretary, with no future prospects. But the first bit was true. There was nothing for me in Scotland. My beloved Balnair would never be truly mine and the man I wanted so badly would soon belong to another woman.

And so, three weeks before his wedding, with my car rammed full of all my worldly belongings, I left.

I'm glad I did that journey alone, as I spent the entirety of the long drive down to Oxford wiping away the endless tears that were streaming down my face. It would have been humiliating if anyone had seen me. By the time I arrived at the estate agents to pick up the keys to the little flat I'd found to rent, I was sure that my face looked like a pufferfish.

But it turned out that Oxford was just what I needed.

It's a city that is busy and bustling. It's full of young

people with dreams and aspirations. My little flat overlooking Magdalen Bridge is cosy and full of character. Don't get me wrong, it's a far cry from the wilds of my beloved Scottish Highlands. Some days, I'll admit that I found myself longing for the open air and empty mountains. But in Oxford, away from Broc, I found contentment.

It was Lily who called me with the news about Broc and Jessica.

My phone rang at 3pm and I frowned when I saw her name.

I knew it was the day of the wedding. With Andy being Broc's best man, I thought the only reason for the call could be that something was wrong with mother.

'Laura, you won't believe it,' Lily had whispered down the phone. 'Jessica never turned up! She did a runner. Poor Broc, he was just standing there and she never arrived. It's all so awkward. I can't talk, I have to go. I'll call you later.'

I'd put my phone in my pocket and looked out the window. Two ducks were floating on the river.

So, Broc wasn't married. Poor guy. He'd have hated being made to look like a fool in front of everyone. I could picture his face with his jaw set hard and his cheeks burning with frustration.

The first thing I asked myself was, should I go back home?

It took me surprisingly little time to find the answer to my own question. No, of course I wouldn't go home. Broc hadn't chosen me. He'd chosen someone else. If he hadn't wanted me before, he wouldn't want me now. Besides, I liked my new home. I liked my job. The people were nice and I was already making friends. No,

I wouldn't go back home.

Of course, I thought of Broc a lot in those first few months. I eagerly scrolled through his Instagram photos, keen to see what he was doing. He didn't post much at first. Heartbroken, I guess. But then he began to post again. And I saw that life was continuing as normal; him and the others, all together. All happy.

I went on loving him from a distance. I did, that was, until the day that Andy died.

I'd always heard that there's a thin line between love and hate. In just a few short hours, I crossed that line. When Broc suddenly became the primary suspect in Andy's murder, I felt a hatred rage inside of me that I've never felt before. I screamed at my phone as I deleted him from my social media, and I tore up all the photos with him in them.

From that moment on, I didn't care about him and I didn't want to know anything about him, or his life.

<u>Continuing the Conversation with Cassie</u>

As Cassie waits for me to answer her, the waiter arrives with our lunch, and it gives me a few moments to gather my thoughts together.

Cassie knows I'd been hopelessly in love with Broc for years. I think half the school had known it. Why wouldn't she assume that I still was? She doesn't know the real reason I moved away, and she probably assumes that Broc and I are still in contact.

Eight months have passed since Andy died and Broc has never been arrested or charged. Unless people know the details of the investigation, they probably assume that he is no longer considered to be a suspect.

'I'm sorry,' says Cassie, once the waiter's gone. 'Was that an insensitive question to ask?'

I smile at her kindly. 'I haven't spoken to Broc for a long time,' I shrug and pick up my spoon. 'Things aren't the same as they used to be.'

I take a mouthful of the Cullen Skink and try my best to savour the creamy, smoky flavour of the fish, but everything is tasteless inside my mouth.

Cassie pokes about at her burger. She's clearly embarrassed to have made me feel awkward.

'I didn't realise, but I should have,' she apologises. 'I didn't even consider him, you know... him being there with Andy and everything.'

'Don't worry,' I say, reaching across the table and

113

patting her on the hand.

I continue eating my soup and Cassie takes a few bites of her burger.

'Are you angry with him?' she asks.

I think about her question for a moment. How on earth can I answer her?

'I feel completely numb towards him,' I reply. 'It's complicated, but that kind of sums it up. I feel nothing.'

It's a lie. I feel a lot. So many different emotions swirl around inside of me when I hear Broc's name, but I'm not going to admit that out loud.

Cassie frowns at me, clearly troubled by my answer.

'Do you think he was responsible for... you know?'

'No. Yes. Maybe.' My thoughts travel back to the conversation I had with George. He doesn't think Broc did it and yet here I am, still undecided.

'Laura, have you spoken to Broc at all since you moved away?'

'No,' I reply, as I stir a chunk of potato around my bowl.

'He's not the same guy he used to be,' she says, and I look up at her.

'What do you mean?' I ask.

'When Jessica left Broc, it broke him. Not him as a person. He's got a personality of steel and he's still full of fiery sarcasm, but it broke his hard, arrogant exterior. He's a different person, or so I hear. My gran told me. Everyone in Foyers loves him, especially the older ones.'

The Broc I remember made a habit of upsetting everyone in the village. This description that Cassie is now giving seems to be of a different person.

'Like I said, it's complicated.' I push my half-eaten lunch

away towards the middle of the table. I've lost my appetite.

Cassie's face is troubled. She reaches out and puts her hand on my arm.

'You know the police have never charged Broc, don't you?' she says.

'Of course, I know that...' I reply, my voice now tensing. 'Sorry, I don't mean to get worked up,' I explain. 'It's just I know a lot more than the general public do about everything. Broc may not have been charged or anything, but he's still on the suspect list.'

'Is he?' Cassie sounds surprised and I nod in response. I then think back to some of the reports I'd read from Inspector Shaw. Initially, Broc was the top suspect but, in reality, there was no evidence to put him above the others.

Cassie interrupts my thoughts, 'You should speak to him.'

'Why?' I ask.

'You need to hear his story, told his way.'

'Do you really think so?' I ask. I don't understand what difference it will make.

Cassie nods. 'I do. He loved Andy like a brother. He spent so much time with your brother and Lily after Jessica left. The three of them grew closer. Gran says that they helped him heal. He's one of your best friends, or at least he used to be. Don't you think you should at least hear what he has to say?'

I don't want to answer her. The last thing I want to do is listen to Broc and his story.

'I'll think about it,' I say, turning my head to watch a group of teenagers skateboarding down the road. I look at my watch. It's almost 2pm and I want to try to see Lily.

'I'm sorry I've not been the best of company,' I say, taking my purse out from my bag. 'I wish I could stay longer but I want to try to visit Lily.'

'How is she getting on?'

'I don't know,' I reply honestly, catching the waiter's eye and waving at him. 'These places never say a lot on the phone. That's why I want to go there in person.'

Cassie nods.

'Poor thing. I came up to Balnair to see her, about two months after it all happened but she refused to see me.'

'I'm not surprised,' I sigh. 'She would barely talk to me when I'd call.'

'Did she ever regain any memory of it all?'

I shift my weight in my seat. It's one thing to talk about me and my feelings about everything but I don't feel comfortable talking to others about Lily.

'I don't know,' I reply, grateful that the waiter has reappeared and is handing me the bill. 'I'll get this. It's my treat,' I say and give him my bank card.

I pay for the lunch and we get up to leave. Cassie takes a step forward and gives me a hug. It's genuine and warm.

'If you see Lily, give her my love,' she says. 'And don't forget what I said about Broc, you should listen to what he has to say.'

I nod in response, although I have absolutely no intention of talking to him.

'It was lovely to see you,' I smile, and we part ways.

Police Interview Between Detective Chief Inspector Shaw (DCIS) and Lilian McClintock (LM)

DCIS: Mrs McClintock. I know that this is very hard for you, but we will try to be a brief as possible. The doctor has informed me that you're suffering from some memory loss which they want to look into further, but I still need to ask you some questions. Can you tell me the last thing you do remember from that afternoon?

LM: I can't remember the afternoon at all. The last memory I have is that I'd just showered and was getting dressed. I wanted to get started on preparing a stew for everyone. Andy popped his head round the bedroom door and said that he was going to take Buddy for a quick walk along the loch before he'd call Laura.

DCIS: Laura is your husband's sister?

LM: Aye.

DCIS: Do you know if your husband called his sister?

LM: I couldn't even tell you if he ever returned from walking the dog. I don't remember anything after that. I'm sorry.

DCIS: Don't worry, Mrs McClintock, I don't want to distress you. So, after that, what is the next thing you remember?

LM: I remember sitting in the lounge with a cup of tea. Father was sitting beside me and there were some policemen in the hall. I looked at the clock and it was lunchtime, but a whole day had passed, it was the twenty-ninth.

DCIS: Were you aware of what had happened?

LM: I must have been, because I didn't ask immediately. But then after a few moments I couldn't understand what was going on, or where Andy was.

DCIS: Mrs McClintock, just take a moment. It's okay. Here's a tissue and some water. I won't ask anything else about the day as you can't remember it, but when you're ready I need to ask a few questions about other things.

LM: I'm alright. I want to get this done quickly. Please, carry on.

DCIS: Are you sure?

LM: I am.

DCIS: In that case, let's continue. Mrs McClintock, how long have you been hunting?

LM: I began shooting in March, when the lockdown began. So, for about nine months now.

DCIS: Have you handled the rifle a lot over that time?

LM: Yes. There hasn't been much else to do, so Andy and I would spend a few mornings a week over on our range, practicing with targets. I used air rifles at first and we would go out looking for small game. Then I moved to the shotgun, and we stepped it up to grouse and pigeons. Finally, he got me on the rifle, and we went for our first stalk together.

DCIS: Have you shot many deer?

LM: Aye, I've shot half a dozen in total now.

DCIS: And would you say that you're comfortable with the rifle?

LM: I am.

DCIS: You load it yourself and everything?

LM: Of course.

DCIS: I want you to imagine that you took a clean shot at a deer at dusk, as the others have said you told them. What would you have done next with your equipment?

LM: If it was the end of the day, I would have made

sure my rifle was safe and then got down from my seat to go to check the kill. If I knew that we were all meeting up by my seat, I would probably wait for the others and then go over to check my kill. Normally, I'd go immediately, but at the end of the day, with the others returning from their seats, it would make sense to wait for a moment.

DCIS: Would your rifle have been reloaded?

LM: Aye, if I was going over to check the kill, I'd most probably have reloaded it. It's standard practice when going to pick up a kill, just in case the initial shot didn't do its job fully.

DCIS: Mrs McClintock. Are you aware that your rifle was reloaded but one of the bullets had been loaded incorrectly?

LM: That's odd.

DCIS: Can you think of a reason you might have done that?

LM: No. As I said, I don't remember anything that I did. Although, if it was dark, maybe I made a mistake.

DCIS: I have a couple more questions about your hunting experience. How accurately can you hit a target at distance?

LM: On the range I'm very accurate up to about three hundred yards, sometimes even more.

DCIS: And out in the field? How far away are your kills usually?

LM: My furthest shot so far is two hundred and fifty yards.

DCIS: The spot you said you shot the deer from was three hundred and fifty yards from your seat.

LM: I'm aware that I said that, but I really can't remember.

DCIS: Okay, let's move on. If you don't mind, I need to ask you about your relationship with Mr McClintock.

LM: Our relationship was fine.

DCIS: How long have you been married?

LM: For about twenty-two months. It would have been two years in February.

DCIS: Were you happy together?

LM: Aye. We were very happy.

DCIS: Are you aware of any issues that your husband may have had with others?

LM: No, everyone loved Andy.

DCIS: What about Mr Henderson? Apparently, he wasn't in a good mood that day?

LM: I can't remember, but, if something was wrong with Broc, I doubt it had anything to do with Andy. They were best friends.

DCIS: Did your husband have financial problems?

LM: No.

DCIS: There have been some recent, regular cash withdrawals from your husband's account. Do you know what they are for?

LM: No. I'm afraid I don't. I wasn't aware of that. How regular and for how much?

DCIS: The money was withdrawn on the last week of the previous three months. Withdrawals of one thousand pounds each time.

LM: That's a lot of money.

DCIS: It is. Are you sure you know nothing about it?

LM: No, I really don't. I'm sorry. I'm a bit surprised by this. Could we take a break?

DCIS: We can finish Mrs McClintock. That was the last thing I needed to ask you about for the moment.

__Failing to See Lily__

It's a short drive across the river to the New Craigs Psychiatric Hospital where Lily is staying.

I pull into the carpark and am relieved to note how pleasant the place looks. I've never visited before and have been filled with dread at what the mental hospital might be like.

Just half a mile down the road is the site of the old, nineteenth-century mental asylum: Craig Dunain Hospital. It closed down over twenty years ago, but as teenagers we used to wander around the deserted grounds, relating made-up stories of the insane patients who had lived there in years gone by. I remember that the old buildings of that asylum were creepy and there was an eerie pond within the grounds. We scared ourselves silly at times with our foolish games and those moments have haunted me since I heard of Lily's admittance to the new hospital only a few weeks ago.

I leave Eileen in one of the parking bays and make my way over to the main reception doors. I checked the visiting guidelines yesterday and so am confident that I'm not arriving at an inconvenient time. I'm feeling hopeful at the prospect of seeing Lily. I've missed her a lot and am desperate to know how she is.

Pulling the elastic ends of my face-covering around my ears, I press the bell at the main reception and wait to be let in. Before long, a woman wearing a nurse's dress and her own clinical face-covering opens the door to me.

'Hi,' I say, smiling and hoping that she'll be able to know

that from the creases at the sides of my eyes. 'I was hoping that I might be able to visit Lilian McClintock.'

'Have you made an appointment?' she asks.

'Err, no,' I reply, my earlier confidence now slipping a little. 'I wasn't entirely sure of my plans and so didn't want to commit to anything.' That's not entirely true. I was worried that if I'd called ahead then Lily might have refused to see me.

She nods at me. 'It shouldn't be a problem. Do you want to come in and sit in our waiting room for a moment while I call through to her ward and find out if it's convenient? Are you family?'

'Yes,' I answer her. 'I'm Laura McClintock, Lily's sister-in-law.'

Her eyes flicker briefly, and I can read her thoughts. She knows I'm Andy's sister and she knows about his death. Of course she does.

I sit down to wait as she disappears along a corridor. I'd originally wondered if they would accept visitors at all, but the restrictions due to the pandemic have eased over recent months and so I'm still hopeful. While she's gone, I take a look around at the waiting area.

The place seems peaceful. It's light and airy and not at all as scary and menacing as I'd expected a mental hospital to be. When Lily was admitted a few weeks ago, I downloaded the patient information sheet and read through it. Everything sounded very nice. The information sheet made it sound a bit like I imagine a retirement village to be, where the residents have access to all sorts of services. Except this place isn't for retired people. It's for sick people. Some of whom are sadly, very sick.

The nurse now returns with someone else following

her. I look up expectantly, assuming it will be Lily, but it's not. It's another member of the medical personnel. I guess that this is someone more superior as she's not in a uniform, but in normal clothes. She's wearing the same sort of medical face-covering as the nurse who had greeted me.

'Miss McClintock,' she says and comes to sit beside me. The other nurse has disappeared. 'It's lovely to meet you. I'm Doctor Fraser, I work on the ward where Lilian is living.'

I look at her. It's so hard to work out people's expressions when half their face is hidden behind a mask, but her eyes are kind.

'Hello,' I reply. 'I was hoping to see Lily. Is she okay?'

'Lily is doing very well. We see gradual improvements in her each day.'

I breathe a sigh of relief. That's good news.

'Am I able to see her?' I ask.

Doctor Fraser lowers her eyes and I clear my throat nervously.

'I'm sorry, but I have to say no to your request,' she answers me. 'When Lily was admitted, we discussed visitation details with her, and she was adamant that she didn't want to see anyone. She especially named her father, her brother and yourself as people that she didn't want to see.'

I can feel tears stinging and threatening at my eyes. I was afraid that this might happen.

Up until two months ago Lily had been communicating with me normally. Well, when I say normally, I mean as normal as possible since Andy died. Lily's not been the same since that day, and understandably so. Life as a young widow, running a large estate, whilst also dealing with the confusion and grief surrounding the circumstances of her husband's death, would have an effect on even the strongest of women. Lily has never been what you would call a 'strong woman' and so she seemed to suffer more than others might have in the same situation.

A few weeks after 'that day' in December, Lily was diagnosed with Localised Dissociative Amnesia. It's a condition that the doctors think was brought on by the tragedy of that afternoon. Lily has no recollection of what happened on that day from the hour of about 9am. Her memory seems to pick back up again at some point the day after. It's like a period of about twenty-four hours has been wiped from her mind. The doctors have told us that while the memories from that day could return, they have no way of knowing when, or even if, they will. Lily may never remember the last time she saw my brother or the last words they said to each other.

Despite the amnesia, Lily and I both remained in fairly frequent contact following Andy's death and I supported her as best I could from the distance I was at. Although she was clearly a woman grieving for the loss of her husband, I thought that she seemed to be coping fairly well.

Then, for no apparent reason, about two months ago, Lily went 'cold turkey' on me. She stopped replying to my messages and avoided my calls, only speaking to me when it was absolutely necessary. I thought I'd done something wrong, but then, as the weeks progressed, it became clear that Lily was slowly losing her grasp of reality and control of her mind. George alerted me to her condition and told me that her doctor was involved. He was quick to get her referred to the New Craigs Hospital and that was the catalyst to me returning home. With Lily gone, and mother in the condition she is in, someone needs to be there, at Balnair.

I don't speak for a moment as I attempt to gather my emotions together. Lily has been my longest and closest friend. It hurts that she's specifically asked not to see me.

Doctor Fraser breaks the silence.

'I'm sorry that you've had a wasted journey,' she says, kindly.

'No. It's not wasted,' I tell her, looking at her gratefully. 'I'm pleased to hear you say that there are improvements. I can go home and give her father some good news. So, it's really not been a wasted journey.'

I move to stand up and she speaks again, 'I'm very sorry for everything that your family have been through.'

'Yes. It's not been an easy time,' I acknowledge. 'Lily's always been a delicate flower, but this has just been too much for her.' I pause, unsure if Lily's refusal to see me means that the doctor can't discuss her condition with me either. I hesitate a moment, but Doctor Fraser doesn't say anything. She seems to be waiting for me to say more and so I carry on talking. 'She was told originally that the amnesia may only be temporary. Do you know if she is remembering things?'

I hold my breath, waiting for her response. I've wondered for a few weeks if the change in poor Lily's mental state has anything to do with her amnesia. Will this kind doctor tell me anything?

'I can't answer that,' she replies, and I feel my shoulders sag a little. Not only is Lily refusing to see me, but I'm also unable able to find out any details about her either. But then Doctor Fraser continues talking. 'She hasn't said anything to us about her memory returning,' she explains. 'All we know is that she is clearly, very, mentally distressed. As you say, she's delicate, but it would seem that there is something else that has triggered the state she is currently in. We're working hard with her to get to the bottom of it. She's not completely broken though. I sense a lot of strength in her. It gives us something to work with.'

This time I breathe a grateful sigh of relief. 'Thank you so much for telling me that. You've been very kind.'

It's true. Doctor Fraser has been kind. I suspect she's spoken more about Lily's condition than she should have. That's sympathy for you. She feels sorry for me. My brother was murdered in the middle of a cold forest, and now my sister-in-law has been admitted to a psychiatric hospital. No doubt, she's also aware of what sadness I face at home with mother. Who wouldn't feel moved to treat me with a touch of compassion and bend the rules of confidentiality a little bit? I know I would, if I were her.

'It's not a problem,' she replies. 'Actually, I was hoping to ask you something, can you think of anything that might have triggered her mind to struggle as it is?'

I shake my head sadly. 'No. I've been in England for the past twenty months. The last time I saw Lily was at my brother's funeral. Since then, we have been in touch on the phone. I did think she was coping reasonably well, but something definitely changed two months ago. What it was, I can't tell you. I'm sorry.'

'It doesn't matter. We'll get to the bottom of it, I'm sure.'

I stand to go.

'Thank you for talking to me,' I say. 'Do you think Lily will want to see me eventually?'

'I'm sure that with time she will,' Doctor Fraser assures me. 'Our aim is to rehabilitate our patients fully back to the life they should have. We just have to take it one day at a time.'

Andy quietly approached Broc's seat and went to climb up.

'Don't move,' hissed Broc.

'You got sight of one?' asked Andy.

Broc nodded. He was holding his binoculars close to his eyes.

'Half a dozen young, red lassies, about one hundred yards away,' he whispered.

Broc slowly lowered the binoculars and pulled the butt of his rifle closer. He placed his left hand under the fore-end and gradually aimed the muzzle where he wanted it.

With his eye looking through the sight, he picked out one of the hinds, choosing the one he could take the cleanest shot at, and then he paused for a moment. Once he was happy that everything was still and under control, Broc released the safety.

The hind heard it. She flinched, and as quickly as his finger could react, Broc pulled the trigger.

The sound of the bullet firing out the barrel shocked the woodland. As soon as the shot was fired, Broc lifted his head up to look ahead. All the deer had disappeared. He checked again with his binoculars. Nothing.

'Blasted thing!' he shouted, pulling the safety back on and sitting back in his seat.

'She's run?' asked Andy.

'Aye, she's run alright. Heard the safety mechanism click, I reckon. I think I missed her.'

'We'll go and check anyway, but we don't want to startle her again. Let's give her a moment or two to calm down after her fright, and then I'll come with you.'

'Andy, come on,' groaned Broc.

'I'd rather check. If it looks like you did hit her, we'll need to try and find her,' insisted Andy.

Broc sighed. He climbed down from his seat and swung his rifle sling around his shoulder. 'Alright then, let's go.'

They walked over to where the hind had been standing when Broc had taken the shot and began to hunt about for traces of blood. Andy soon found some on the ground.

'We'll start from here,' he said. 'Which way did she run?'

Broc pointed ahead and they both moved forwards.

'If they all ran together it'll be easy, but if they've broken up and separated from each other, we'll struggle to keep on her trail,' said Broc, as they passed some broken branches and another spot of blood.

'Wait a moment. We haven't told the others were trailing one,' said Andy, coming to a standstill. 'Give me your radio, I'll let them know.'

Broc patted his coat pockets and then sighed. 'I've left it on top of my bag, at the seat. You've got yours though, haven't you?'

'Yeh, but I'm not sure how well it's working.'

Andy called into his radio, letting the others know that he and Broc were trailing a deer. There was no reply. He tried again. Just faint crackling could be heard in the receiver.

'What do you want to do? Go back?' asked Broc, hopeful that Andy would decide not to try and track the injured deer after all. It would normally be Broc's automatic response to go after any and every hit, but today he didn't want to. He didn't want to be anywhere near Andy.

'No, we're heading away from the range of the others already. It looks as though she's run down the hill towards the clearing. We're not in any danger here. We'll just have to make sure that we come back up from the other side.'

They continued walking in silence, both looking for disturbed ground, blood and any other evidence of where the injured deer had headed. Andy knew something was wrong with Broc. He could sense it in his demeanour.

'Is something bothering you, mate?' he asked, bending down to check another drop of blood on the ground.

Broc's eyes were steely and he stared ahead without replying.

'Broc?'

Broc looked at Andy and stopped walking.

'What's going on with you and Ailish?' he asked. Broc's voice was calm, but Andy could see that his fists were clenched.

Andy felt his face heat up in response to the question.

'Nothing,' he shrugged and moved forwards to examine another broken branch. 'Why do you ask?'

'I saw you both yesterday, out by the gateway to the southern plantation.'

'She needed my advice on something,' said Andy, still looking at the branch.

'Must have been some five-star advice you gave her judging by the embrace I saw you both in.' Broc's words were simple, but his tone of voice was laden with accusation.

Andy felt a cold, fluttery feeling weave its way across his chest.

'It's not what you think!' he replied, turning to look at his friend.

'If it's not what I think, then perhaps you could explain to me exactly what it is.'

Broc rested his hand against his gun to steady it as it moved on his shoulder. Andy suddenly felt uneasy. Broc hated deception of any sort and Andy knew he would have to choose his words carefully, or his friend would not like it.

'It's not really my place to say anything,' Andy answered him, holding his hands out in a display of honesty. 'It's something private to Ailish, and I gave her my word that I'd not talk about it. Not to anyone.'

Andy held his breath. Ailish had been very upset yesterday and she had clung onto him for what had felt like an age. If Broc had witnessed that, then Andy knew the sort of assumptions he would have come to. He hoped that his answer would be enough to stop Broc from asking any more questions: questions that he couldn't answer, not at least until he'd had a chance to speak to Lily.

Broc didn't say anything for a moment. He just stared hard at Andy's face, glaring into his eyes, trying to read what was truly going on. Then he moved forwards.

'Let's just find this deer, shall we?' he said, and walked on, following the trail.

Alone with a Few Drams

I can feel myself losing the will to live as I weave my way up and down the aisles at Tesco. Eventually, I'm loading several heavy shopping bags into the back of Eileen. I'm exhausted. It's been a hard day emotionally and now my body is starting to protest too as my joints moan painfully with each movement I make.

On the drive back to Balnair, my head is in a bit of a haze. It's one of those drives when you suddenly realise that you're not really concentrating and can't remember the previous twenty minutes of the journey, let alone recall the things you're passing along the way, and then you scare yourself with the reality of how dangerous that is.

As Eileen and I climb up the hill, back towards home, the bright sunshine, that has been with me for most of the day, disappears. Low, grey clouds begin to roll in and, by the time the loch comes into view, I've already turned the wipers on, as a steady drizzle begins to fall from the sky. This is the Highlands I know. I shake my head to myself and pull into the driveway.

Eventually, I've unloaded all the shopping and fed Buddy his tea. It's now time to set about making myself something to eat. I'm starving. My stomach has recovered from its earlier loss of appetite and is now making loud noises at me as a way of hinting that it's past feeding time.

Too tired to start chopping onions and preparing, what I call, a 'real meal', I pull two trays out from the cupboard. One I load with a frozen pizza and the other with frozen chips. This will have to do for tonight.

Julie is on duty again this evening and she comes into the kitchen to prepare mother's meal. It's something that Andy had included as part of the arrangements for mother's care package, but it feels weird to me: someone else making a meal for your own mother. I know that it had made a lot of practical sense for Andy and Lily though. Sometimes he would be caught up with things on the estate until late into the evening and Lily would often be with him. Mother needs a regular routine, and they hadn't been able to keep to that.

Julie smiles and makes happy conversation with me whilst she heats the dinner which has been defrosting on the side during the day. I feel really uneasy but realise that she doesn't see anything abnormal in this set up. For now, I'm not making any adjustments to mother's care schedule, but I know that at some point I'll need to decide on how I want to go ahead with everything in a way that will work for me.

The timer goes off on the oven and, gratefully, I push those thoughts to one side. They can wait for another day.

After loading a plate with the cardboard looking pizza and beige-coloured chips, I follow Julie as she carries mother's plate of Shepherd's Pie through to her drawing room.

'I'll join you for dinner, if that's alright with you,' I say, pulling a chair out opposite mother at her small dining table.

She looks at me and smiles. Her eyes are vacant and glassy.

'How delightful,' she replies and then focuses her attention onto her plate of food.

The mealtime passes both slowly and silently. Julie politely sits to one side in an armchair and gets on with reading a book. Is she judging me for not making conversation with my own mother? I don't know. But it's hopeless. I can't think of a single question to put to her that might be 'safe' to ask. I'm even afraid of calling her mother in case it causes any upset.

Eventually mother finishes her meal and I stand up to clear both of our plates. I can feel Julie's eyes watching me.

'Perhaps you would like to look at some photos with us, Laura,' she says, as I'm about to leave the room with the dirty crockery.

I look up at her in surprise.

'Mrs McClintock often likes to look back through the photo albums after she's had her dinner,' continues Julie, 'And of course, it's always nice to have some company.'

Nodding at the suggestion, I put the tray of plates down.

Looking at photos is something mother has always enjoyed doing. Each year, she had carefully and lovingly made a photo album and now there are many sitting on a shelf in the cupboard. Julie explains to me that they regularly look through them together. Julie purposefully avoids the albums that cover the most recent years, with the memories that have now faded from mother's mind. Instead, she picks albums that go back many decades, to times and people that mother can remember. To my surprise, I find that I enjoy looking at the albums too. It's nice to see old photos of my parents at a time before I was born.

Before too long, it's time for mother to go to bed and I

say goodnight to her, allowing Julie to escort her to her room.

After washing up the dishes and tidying the kitchen, I make my way to the main lounge and turn on the T.V. Buddy immediately pads his way over, jumps up onto the sofa and sprawls out next to me. He'd never been allowed to do that when I lived here before, but I guess things have changed in my absence. Flicking through the channels, I stop as I see a scene I recognise. It's of one of the colleges in Oxford, I'm sure of it. Bringing up the menu, I can see that I've inadvertently stumbled across a replay of an old episode of Morse. Finally, I can learn what the hype is about with this programme.

Pulling my feet up underneath myself, I'm about to settle down when a quick glance across at the whisky cabinet distracts me for a moment.

'Why not? No one else is going to drink it,' I think to myself as I stand back up, get a glass and open the doors.

Father had amassed an exquisite whisky collection over the years and Andy had also added a few of his own to it. Having just looked through endless photos of my dear father in his prime as a healthy, young man, I'm now feeling somewhat nostalgic. My father had always been a fan of Dalmore and their whisky. The distillery is local, and he liked to support local things. My eyes rest on a bottle of Dalmore 'Port Wood' which had also become a favourite of Andy's in recent years. Without hesitating, I reach for the bottle, pour myself a generous measure and then take both the bottle and the glass back to the sofa.

As I'm watching John Thaw walk through the iconic grounds of Oxford's colleges alongside his on-scene companion Kevin Whately (better known as, 'Lewis'), I take a sip of the smooth single malt. The liquid in my hand is rich in colour. It reminds me of the trademark McClintock hair: a sort of sun-kissed rum mixed with cherrywood orange. Flavours of fruity caramel begin to swirl around my mouth, and I savour it.

I was raised being forced to appreciate the subtle delights of this drink which made my country so famous. As a young adult, I learned that whisky tasting is an art, and no mouthful should ever be gulped down in haste. I continue sipping away at the Dalmore, pouring myself a second helping, while also attempting to pick up the story on the T.V. Having missed the beginning, it takes a moment, but I soon learn that an Oxford Don has committed suicide. Watching as Morse speaks with the grieving widow reminds me again of poor Lily and the state that she is in.

Of course, there is nothing for Lily to feel guilty about. Her and Andy had a happy relationship. It wasn't like they'd been miserable together or that he'd become fed up with life. My brother hadn't committed suicide like the man on the T.V. He'd not even taken his rifle with him that day. Andy had insisted that he wasn't interested in the deer that day, but really just wanted an excuse for a bit of normality with his friends, following nine months of pressures from a life under the restrictions of the pandemic. But that desire for something nice for everyone had turned into something awful.

I reach out for the bottle and go to pour myself a third glass. My fingers graze against the raised, silver engraving on the bottleneck and I stare at it for a moment. The Dalmore Stag. It's the iconic mark of their whisky.

Suddenly my mouth tastes sour as I look at the image and thoughts of Andy and the others, out on the estate with their rifles, fill my head. This impressive creature represents something prestigious for the customers and drinkers of this whisky, but, for me, it represents something else. It represents death, betrayal, lies and loss.

Feeling a hatred for the Dalmore, I stand up and return it to the cabinet, placing it firmly at the back, out of sight. Instead, I pick up a 'Port Charlotte Heavily Peated' from the Bruichladdich distillery. It's one of my own favourites. I'm a traitor to the Highlands when it comes to my preference in single malt. The peaty flavours of the Islay's suit my palate much better than many others. I pour some into my glass, careful not to pour too much. I can feel my emotions are already high and I don't want to push myself over the edge by drinking more than is wise. The liquid of this whisky is much paler than the Dalmore had been. You might assume from appearances alone that it is weaker in some way, but that's deceptive. As I lift the glass towards my nose, a scent of earthy iodine and TCP travels up my nostrils. I hesitate for a moment. Do I love this whisky as much as I think I do? Then I take a mouthful and smile. Yes, I really do love it. The strong, almost burnt, flavours instantly hit the back of my mouth and I feel my senses explode into life. I then sink back into the sofa as all the peaty harshness melts into a gentle, soft, honey-like delicacy and leaves a warm glow inside my mouth.

With the dram of Port Charlotte in my hand I try to re-focus on the programme, but my mind refuses to do so. My thoughts flick back instead to my conversation with Cassie. She'd told me that Broc has changed. She'd urged me to speak to Broc, even insinuating that I owe it to him to do so.

I don't owe Brochan Henderson anything, but I'll admit that there are questions still begging for answers.

Fired up by the bonfire that is going on inside my mouth, I put the glass down and reach for my phone. I soon find Broc's name on my list of WhatsApp contacts. The profile picture is of him and his brother. It must have been taken almost fifteen years ago. They are standing at the top of some mountain and the view behind them is amazing.

Without stopping to hesitate or change my mind, I tap on the message box and begin writing.

'Andy, will you just admit it? We've lost the trail. Let's come back out in the morning with one of the dogs and pick her up,' suggested Broc, leaning his hand against the trunk of a tree.

They were at the bottom of the hill, on the edge of a small clearing. There was an open stretch of about fifteen hundred yards between them and the west plantation. They'd not seen any spots of blood for a while. Andy, still poking about in the undergrowth, stopped and looked up.

'You're right, I don't think we'll find her.'

'We should have left her in the first place. Now we're the wrong side of the woods and it's almost sunset.'

Andy didn't reply. When Broc was in a mood like this, it wasn't worth it, especially as the reason for his mood was directed towards him.

'We'll head back then,' said Andy. Broc had already begun to walk in the direction they'd come from when Andy stopped him. 'No. We can't be sure my radio is working, remember? We'll have to follow the perimeter round and then go up past the back of the others. It's the only safe way.'

Broc sighed. It would take at least thirty minutes to get back to his seat and his bag. Broc began walking again and then stopped as he realised that Andy still wasn't following him.

'Are you coming?'

'I just thought, I have a few traps down by the fence line over there,' Andy replied. 'I might as well check them while I'm here. If you go on ahead, I'll just make my way back to Lily when I done, unless you want to come with me?'

'I'll go on. My stuff is still at my seat. If I come with you, I'll be ages getting everything.'

139

Andy nodded. Broc was in such a bad mood, and he felt like it was his fault. 'I'm sorry mate.'

Broc shrugged and walked off, his rifle swinging in its sling.

Andy did feel bad. He knew Broc hadn't wanted to go after the deer and yet he'd made him. But Broc would get over it. He never stayed in a bad mood for long. Not like Will, who took weeks to forgive even the smallest mistakes. He'd need to apologise to Will for being so short with him too. Andy rubbed the back of his neck as he made his way across the clearing to check the two traps. The sun was setting, but there was nothing much spectacular to look at. The clouds were obscuring any colourful show that the sky might have put on, on a different day.

The traps were empty, and so Andy walked back to the edge of the woods.

The afternoon hadn't really gone as he had hoped it would. Still, Lily had prepared a really good stew for them all. He hoped that once they got back to the house and everyone was sitting around the firepit with hot food and a whisky or two inside them, that it would all be okay.

As Andy walked, something on the ground caught his eye and he stopped. He bent down and touched it. Blood. Fresh blood.

He looked up. This wasn't the same area where they had walked earlier. Perhaps the injured hind had come out, onto the clearing for a moment and then dropped back into the safety and security of the woodland.

To his right, further into the woodland, Andy could see what looked like broken branches. He went over and to his delight, he found more blood on the ground. He smiled to himself. He was back on the trail. Maybe they could find this missing deer after all.

Meeting with Broc

I stir and roll over in my bed. It's already light and I've slept through yet another full night of sleep. I could get used to this.

My first thought is of the message I sent last night. Reaching across for my phone, I can see that a response is waiting for me. Broc had replied about thirty minutes ago.

I'd heard you were back. Wanted to get in touch but wasn't sure if I should. I'm really pleased to hear from you. How about we meet for a drink later this afternoon? Dores? B

My hands shake as I read his words. It's not that I regret contacting him. No, I think that a conversation about everything, and hopefully some answers, will be good for me. It's more that my message to him last night had been full of courage: 'Dutch Courage'. I read over what I'd written to him again.

Hi Broc. Laura here. I'm home at the moment, at Balnair. I'd like to see you if possible. I need to ask you some questions. Let me know when you're free.

I'm impressed with myself. I used to tiptoe around Broc, doing anything I could to try and please him. To try and get him to take notice of me. To try and get him to love me. The message I sent last night comes across as quite aloof. I sound cool, calm, and confident. Now though, knowing that in just a few hours' time I will see Broc in the flesh, I feel anything but calm. Last night's courage has faded and I'm trembling inside.

After lunch, I spend almost an hour trying to replicate the nonchalant tone of my message in my appearance. I pathetically change and un-change my clothing about a dozen times in a vain attempt to find something that makes me look casual and yet fabulous at the same time. It's certainly not that I want Broc to fancy me or fall in love with me. Too much water has passed under that bridge. I don't crave his love anymore like I used to, but I do want him to see that I'm doing just fine without him in my life. And it would definitely be a feather in my cap if I could make him regret not choosing me.

In the end I go for my dungarees with a bright t-shirt underneath. My dungarees are a flattering, modern, high-leg style. They have the ability to lengthen the appearance of my own legs, which is hard to do in someone my height. I can already feel myself shrinking in apprehension of what is to come, so any help to make me look taller is welcome.

Finally, with a stomach full of nerves, it's time for me to go.

I give my own car an apologetic glance as I once again get into the driving seat of Eileen. Something about driving her makes me feel like Andy is still with me, and I like that feeling.

It's still damp outside, and the midges are swarming. Clouds of them are swiped across the windscreen as the wipers go back and forth. I'm glad I've popped a bottle of 'Smidge' in my bag. I'll need some repellent if we're going to sit on a bench by the water.

The journey passes too quickly and, before I feel ready for it, I've arrived.

Although it's a bit of a drive back along Loch Ness, I'm glad that Broc suggested we meet at Dores. It's neutral ground. I feel that meeting somewhere neutral is very important for me right now.

Dores is a little inn next to Dores Beach on Loch Ness. Popular with both visitors and locals, they serve good food and drink, surrounded by beautiful views (on a clear day). As I pull into the carpark there is still a misty drizzle falling onto the car windows. I reach over the passenger seat for my jacket. It's muggy, but I don't fancy getting wet.

I get out of the car and walk towards the pub. Broc is already there. He's standing just inside the small doorway at the entrance to the inn, waiting for me. He's looking at his phone and so doesn't notice me approaching.

Involuntarily, my breath catches in my throat when I see him there. Despite everything, I realise that I'm still incredibly attracted to him. He's not shaved for what looks like a week or two, and the stubble suits him. It highlights his strong cheekbones. He's wearing a pair of jeans and a t-shirt. His muscular arms are tanned from being outdoors all summer.

It's been twenty months since I last saw Broc and yet, looking at him now, it feels like only yesterday. A short, wave of annoyance sweeps through me as I realise that, despite the distance and separation, my insides still turn to jelly at the sight of this guy.

Broc glances up and catches sight of me. I falter for a moment as emotions threaten to frighten me away, but then I regain my strength and continue walking towards him.

'Wee Ginge,' he says. His voice is soft, and meek. He holds his arms out, hopeful of a hug.

'Hi Broc,' I reply, keeping my arms firmly at my side. 'Thanks for coming.'

He nods, clearly crestfallen at my cold manner. It hurts me too, but I can't break, not yet anyway. I need to stay focused on why I'm here.

He goes to open the door for me, and I pause. The wretched 'covid anxiety' has stopped me in my steps.

'Would you mind if we sit outside?' I ask.

Broc looks up at the sky. 'In this weather?'

'The tables have a marquee covering them,' I shrug.

Broc contemplates what I've said and then nods. 'You go and sit down. I'll get us some drinks,' he says.

I walk over to a table and sit down. No one else is sitting outside. I realise that's probably a good thing. I don't really want eavesdroppers on the conversation that Broc and I are about to have.

He soon emerges from the inn carrying two drinks and sits down opposite me at the table. He's bought me a rum and coke. I take a sip from my glass.

'Thank you,' I say and pull the collar of my jacket up around my neck a little. I can feel his eyes watching me.

'Is it still your favourite, or have your tastes changed while you've been away?' he asks, with a tone in his voice that raises a heat rash on my neck.

I take another gulp of my drink and avoid eye contact with him as I lose all focus on the flavours inside my mouth and am sure that he's not making reference to my drink either.

As if to confirm what I'm thinking, he speaks again. 'You look amazing, Laura.'

I keep my eyes fixed on the glass in my hands. For years I'd wanted him to tell me I looked amazing, but now it's too late. Like I said earlier, too much water has flowed under that bridge.

'I love your hair. It's like copper. And it's so long. You should never have started to dye it all those years ago. You didn't suit blonde. It wasn't very... you.'

If only he knew that I'd dyed it blonde all those years just to try and get his attention.

I still won't make eye contact and he stops talking. There's an awkward pause between us.

'So why did you want to see me,' he asks. His voice has fallen flat from my deliberate refusal to take part in his small talk.

'I don't know,' I reply. It's partly true. I'm not really sure why I want to see him, except that I think that he could possibly have some answers for me. 'I guess I've just been thinking about everything and, well, I had lunch with Cassie, you remember her, don't you?' He nods. 'She suggested that I should speak to you personally. That I should hear everything from your own mouth. Give you a chance, I suppose.'

'Is that what you want?' asks Broc, staring hard at me. 'To give me a chance?'

I look away for a moment, unable to hold his intense look. Then I resolve to be strong and to be firm. Looking back at him, I attempt to meet his eyes with some confidence. But it's no good. I'm not fooling anyone.

'Let's see,' I shrug, giving away just how hopeless I feel

the situation is. 'Tell me your story of what happened to Andy.'

BH: I just explained to you! I left my radio at my seat and Andy's wasn't working properly. I was about to go back for mine, but he said not to worry.

DCIS: Mr Henderson, do you need a moment to calm down?

BH: No, I'm sorry. I don't mean to get frustrated. I know you need to ask these questions. Sorry. I'll be calmer.

DCIS: I just need to understand if this was a normal thing to do, to go after a kill with no radio.

BH: No, it wasn't. Andy said not to worry though as we were out of the range of the others, and to be honest, I was in such a bad mood that I didn't care.

DCIS: Why were you in a bad mood?

BH: This doesn't sound good, but I was upset with Andy.

DCIS: Over what?

BH: I'd seen something that I didn't like.

DCIS: What did you see? Mr Henderson, I need you to tell me why you were upset with Mr McClintock.

BH: The day before, I'd seen him with Ailish. They were... close. I thought something was going on with them both.

DCIS: You mean you think that Mr McClintock was having an affair with Miss Briars?

BH: Yes... No... I don't know.

DCIS: Did you ask Mr McClintock about it?

BH: I did. I asked him while we were together, trailing the deer. He just said that he couldn't tell me what was going on between them. I didn't ask anything else.

DCIS: What do you think now?

BH: I can't believe that Andy would have done anything like that to Lily, but I just don't know.

DCIS: Were Mr and Mrs McClintock happy together?

BH: Aye. They were. I actually used to be a bit of envious of what they had.

DCIS: You and Mr McClintock have been friends for a long time, haven't you?

BH: We've been best friends for as long as I can remember. He was almost like a brother to me.

DCIS: If someone we're that close to lets us down or disappoints us, it can make us very angry.

BH: Wait a minute. You think I'd have killed him because I was a bit upset with him? I'd never do that. I'd never kill anyone, let alone Andy, of all people!

DCIS: Mr Mitchell claims it was you.

BH: William Mitchell doesn't like me.

DCIS: Why not?

BH: For lots of reasons. I tease him too much. I know I do. He hates being teased. And he never forgets anything. If someone upsets him, he holds on to it. He's never liked me much. He blames me for Laura moving away.

DCIS: That's Mr McClintock's sister?

BH: Aye.

DCIS: Why does he blame you for that?

BH: I don't know. He just accused me once. Told me it was my fault that she left, but it wasn't. He was just being emotional. Laura left Scotland because she found a job in England. I didn't have anything to do with it. I was as surprised

DCIS: as everyone else when she said she was going.

DCIS: So, you say that Mr Mitchell is lying?

BH: Of course he is!

DCIS: Is he lying about seeing you near the lower seat?

BH: No. That is true.

DCIS: Why were you there?

BH: Andy and I followed that trail until we lost it. By then, we were on the opposite side of the woods, right down at the lower end of the hill. The quickest way to return safely to my seat was to track around the perimeter. I would have walked past the back of the seat where Lily and Will were, and that must be when Will saw me.

DCIS: But at that point you were alone?

BH: Aye. Andy went to check some traps on the other side of the woodland, but I continued on. It was almost sunset, and I had a long way to go to get back to my seat.

DCIS: Did you see anyone else while you were with Mr McClintock?

BH: No.

DCIS: When was the last time you saw Mr McClintock?

BH: When he went to check the traps.

DCIS: Did you hear the last two shots?

BH: Aye.

DCIS: Where were you when they were fired?

BH: I was probably not very far from where William had seen me when I heard the first one. Then George Thompson and I heard the last one as we were walking back down the woodland together.

149

DCIS: Did you see anyone else moving about at that time?

BH: No.

DCIS: Can I just confirm the following: Miss Briars, Mrs McClintock and you have all admitted to taking shots that afternoon. The two women claim they each cleanly hit a deer and you claimed to have missed your target?

BH: That's correct.

DCIS: You all claimed to have taken your shots from your seats.

BH: Aye.

DCIS: At the end of the afternoon, Mr McClintock's body and that of a deer were found in the area claimed to have been aimed at by the two women?

BH: Sadly, yes.

DCIS: Did you ever find your runaway deer?

BH: No, I didn't. I was going to go back with the dogs, but you lot won't let me near the place. Aren't your people looking for it? Can't they find it?

DCIS: Yes, they have been looking for it, and no they can't find it. It's a shame, Mr Henderson. That missing deer appears to be the alibi you need to find.

BH: Did anyone find the other deer that was claimed to be shot by either Lily or Ailish?

DCIS: No. But the deer we did find at the scene had a second wound, so it appears the two women most probably took shots at the same deer. It's probable that Miss Briars injured it and that Mrs McClintock killed it.

Mr Henderson, the last time that Mr McClintock is confirmed, by more than one person, as being alive was when he radioed to tell you that he was walking from Miss Briar's seat to your seat. Can you give any evidence that he arrived at your seat and that you fired, as you said, at a deer from your seat?

BH: Are you saying that you think I'm lying?

DCIS: Without witnesses or evidence, it's quite probable that you could have left your seat and shot Mr McClintock before he got to you. You were aware that he was on his way towards you. You could easily have lured him as close as possible to the area around Miss Briars' seat in order to frame one of the others. Luckily for you that the deer was shot almost exactly in the same place as where you dumped the body.

BH: Do you really think that's what happened?

DCIS: Well, it ties in with what Mr Mitchell saw and the location of Mr McClintock's body would certainly make my theory a likely possibility.

BH: An unlikely possibility, if you ask me! He was found the other side of Ailish's seat to where I was positioned.

DCIS: Unlikely, maybe. But still possible, nevertheless.

BH: No sir. Impossible, I'm afraid.

DCIS: Why do you say that?

BH: Because I loved Andy like he was my own brother.

DCIS: Mr Henderson, that may be true, but do you have any evidence to support your version of the story?

BH: I would have, if your guys could find the bullet that killed him. I homeload all my own gear. If you find that bullet, you'll see that it's not mine.

DCIS: We are working on that. Alright, Mr Henderson, back to that afternoon. At the end of the day, when you all met back together, did anyone seem suspicious to you?

BH: Not really. Ailish was the last to arrive back to the meeting point. I did think it odd that her and Lily claimed to have taken a kill in almost the same spot in a fairly short space of time, but it's not impossible. Their seats weren't far apart from each other and there would have been an area of ground covered by both positions.

DCIS: What was everyone's reaction when you all came across Mr McClintock on the ground?

BH: It's all a bit of a blur, but I remember a lot of noise and confusion, along with crying from the girls, of course.

DCIS: And it was at this point that Mr Mitchell accused you, was it?

BH: Aye. He shouted that it was me and then he ran off.

DCIS: Where did he go?

BH: He ran back towards the seat, but then when we got back there, he'd gone. He was nowhere to be seen.

DCIS: Did you see anyone moving the rifles and hunting equipment?

BH: No. George took charge of everything. He called 999 and told us to leave everything exactly where it was.

DCIS: Who was carrying their rifle at that point?

BH: Just me. I'd taken mine up to check the kill. We'd left everything else behind.

DCIS: Thank you, Mr Henderson. We'll take a break now.

Hearing Broc Out

I somehow manage to listen patiently as Broc carefully explains to me the events of that afternoon from his point of view.

'Laura, you have to understand. I loved Andy like he was my own brother.' Broc says, holding his palms up on the table. 'He might as well have been my brother too after, well, you know, after what happened to Shane. Andy was my best pal. There's no way I'd ever have done anything to him.'

Broc stops talking and looks at me. His eyes are pleading with me to believe him, and I think I do. I've never known Broc tell a lie in his life, and he hates it when others do. It makes him angrier than anything else.

A memory from the past suddenly comes to me. It was years ago, when Andy and Broc had returned one year from university. Andy, for some unknown reason, told Broc a lie. I don't even remember what it was about now, but I can remember clearly Broc's response to it. He punched Andy hard, right on his left eye. I saw it and can remember gasping out loud at the violence that emitted from Broc in those few seconds against his best friend. They were talking again within a day or two and Andy told me that he'd deserved it, and he didn't blame Broc for the action, but it was something that had left me shocked me for a while.

Yes, honesty has always been an important quality to Broc and now, more than ever, he wants me to trust his honesty. I can see the desperation in his face and so I compassionately reach my hand out and touch his lightly.

'I believe you, Broc. I do,' I tell him, my voice choking a little as I realise that I'm not lying.

'You do?' he asks, as his own voice cracks in return.

Upon reflection, I'm not sure if I ever really thought of Broc as a genuine suspect for Andy's murder. I was just angry when I found out that was what the police thought. But even they're not sure now.

I nod in response to his question, and he squeezes my hand gently. The result of this contact is a tingling sensation that travels up my arm and makes my back quiver. I pull my hand away quickly.

'So, if it wasn't you, then who was it?' I ask.

Broc's face clouds over.

'It's so hard to work that out. I've gone back and forth in my head for months, but I still can't make sense of it.'

'That's what George said when I asked him the same question,' I say, picking up my glass and taking in a mouthful of my drink. Our drinks had been abandoned whilst Broc was talking. He now mirrors me and lifts his own glass to his mouth too. Placing it back on the table, he begins to speak again.

'Do you trust George?'

'Of course,' I say, without hesitation.

'And now you trust me?' he checks.

I nod.

'What about Lily?' he asks.

I shake my head. 'It's not Lily. I don't care what anyone says, Lily would never...' I can't finish the sentence, and so stop talking.

'It's okay. I agree with you.' Broc's voice is kind. 'So, that leaves only two people, and both of them seem suspicious to me,' he says, looking into the, now empty, pint glass in his hand. He pauses, as if wondering whether it's wise to say their names out loud or not. Finally, he says it. 'Will and Ailish.' His voice is quiet, as if just saying their names might convict them of the horrible crime.

I shake my head in response.

'I don't see how that's possible,' I respond, fervently.

'Well, Will is clearly lying about something. He certainly lied when he told them it was me!'

A family walk past where we're sitting, and the father looks at us, concerned that something is amiss. Broc is emotional, I can tell. He's speaking with a raised voice. I give the man a smile to assure him that all is well, and then say nothing for a moment, allowing Broc some time to settle.

'Why do you think Will did say it was you?' I ask him eventually, once the family are out of earshot.

Broc shrugs. 'To cover up the truth? Because he doesn't like me? I don't know.'

'What makes you think that Will doesn't like you?' I'm confused now.

'He's always had something against me. Probably because I was always teasing him.' I nod in agreement. Broc lowers his eyes and continues, 'Anyway, I've felt for a while that he doesn't like me, especially after you left. It's like he blames me for you moving away.'

I feel my cheeks blush and I quickly lift my glass and finish my drink. If Will does blame Broc for me leaving, then he's right, but I don't want Broc to know that.

'Will doesn't even have a gun though,' I point out, steering the subject back towards the hunt.

'No, but his prints were all over Lily's, weren't they? And he won't tell the police why.'

'But even if he did, for some reason, touch Lily's gun, he's never fired a rifle. I don't think he'd even know how to, let alone be able to aim the thing at a target!' I protest, adamant that Will couldn't have done it.

I fall silent for a moment, and attempt to take in everything that Broc is saying. I don't like to think that Will, Andy's sweet, innocent brother-in-law, might be the one responsible for his death. But then, I feel my own face pale as I suddenly remember something.

'What is it?' asks Broc. He can see that something is disturbing me.

'I found a letter,' I admit. 'It's from Will, written to Lily. For some reason he thought that Andy was making Lily's life miserable. Do you think that would make him want to kill Andy?'

Broc thinks for a moment.

'Will's mind doesn't work like the rest of ours, so I guess anything is possible.' Broc pauses to think for a moment and then shakes his head and continues talking. 'Lily wasn't miserable though. She and Andy loved each other.'

'So, they were happy?' I ask, 'leading up to.... everything.'

'Yes, of course they were,' Broc confirms, and I close my eyes as I feel a rush of relief travel through me. Since reading that letter, I've been overcome with worry that something might have been amiss between Andy and

Lily. When I open my eyes though, the relief flees from me. I can see that it's now Broc's face that has gone white.

'What? What is it?' I insist.

'It's Ailish,' he replies, pausing slightly. 'There was something going on with her and Andy.'

'What do you mean?'

'I don't know. I asked him about it and he wouldn't give me a straight answer.'

'But you have an idea of what it was, do you?'

Broc looks away. His face is pained slightly by whatever it is that he's about to say.

'Laura, I saw them clinging to each other... in a way that didn't seem right.'

He watches me carefully as I take in what he's implying.

'You mean, you think something was going on between them, like some sort of affair?' I ask, not quite believing what I'm hearing.

Broc doesn't respond.

'Broc, I know Ailish. I know her better than anyone,' I tell him. 'And I knew my brother too. Something like that would never happen!'

'I hear you Laura, I do. But if there's one thing I've learned from that whole thing with Jessica, it's that you never really know people.'

I nod and realise that what he is saying is true. We never truly know what people are capable of, even if we think we know them really well.

We're both silent for a moment and I take the opportunity to gather my thoughts a bit.

I'm not even sure if what we're doing is right: the two of us, sitting here discussing it all and the people involved like we are. We're going over everything as if it's some plot in an Agatha Christie novel. It feels wrong, but now we've started, I don't want to stop.

It's actually doing me some good, this process of dissecting things and pulling it all apart, as if it were a poor frog in one of our biology lessons at school. Having this conversation with Broc is helping my mind to deal with everything.

For so long, I've been distant from it all, drawing my own conclusions based on what small snippets of information I've been given. But now, here, talking to Broc, who, up until fifteen minutes ago, had been high on my hit list; it's helping me. It's helping me to cope with it all. Being with Broc is helping me to cope.

I realise how crazy that is.

'What made you send that message last night,' asks Broc, as if reading my mind.

I think back to the fiery courage I'd been given by the drop of Port Charlotte I drank yesterday evening. 'A dram or two from father's collection,' I admit, smiling a little. Broc returns it with a warm smile of his own.

I can feel my head going giddy. I'm losing grasp of the steely exterior that I've been determined to maintain whilst with him.

'I'm sorry about Jessica,' I blurt out.

'No, you're not,' he smirks.

I've always wondered if Andy ever told Broc the real reason I left.

'It was never going to work' he shrugs, 'I see that now,

in hindsight. The poor girl didn't know the head of a sheep from its tail,' he laughs. 'There was never going to be a 'Highland, happily-ever-after' there'.

I look down at my hands. I'd always hoped that Broc would be my *'Highland-happily-ever after'*, but that boat sailed a long time ago.

28th December 2020

3:47pm

Will had his own pair of binoculars.

For most of the afternoon, he'd sat at the bottom of the seat, facing the opposite direction to Lily, and looked through them. Earlier he'd been watching the squirrels as they played, running around at the tops of the trees.

He put the binoculars down and was listening to the growling of his hungry stomach when he saw a movement between the trees.

Watching closely, he saw that it was Broc. Will could see that Broc was carrying his gun in its sling and that he was moving fast, as though in a hurry.

Will frowned to himself.

What was Broc doing down here in this area? He'd gone to a seat much further up the woodland with George.

Will lifted his binoculars. It was beginning to get dark, but he could still see Broc's face clearly. Broc looked annoyed, the same expression he'd had earlier, back at the house, only now it was a bit more so.

Will didn't care too much for Broc. He'd always felt that the other man didn't like him, and Will certainly didn't like the way Broc treated him, or others. He didn't like the way Broc had treated Laura. Will felt that if he was Broc, and Laura had paid him the amount of attention she paid to Broc, then Will would definitely have treated her nicely.

As Broc disappeared out of sight, another rumble came from Will's stomach, and he took out a chocolate bar from his pocket and began to unwrap it.

Taking Everything In

We say goodbye and I open the door to Eileen, pretending to get in. Once Broc's car has disappeared from sight, I get out, shut the door behind me and walk back towards the inn. Beyond the tables, is the small beach which lays alongside Loch Ness. The clouds have now lifted a little and I feel as though I need a walk. My head is spinning like a washing machine and a bit of alone time is needed to settle it down.

In the corner of the carpark is a converted van, called 'The Spot', which sells fresh coffee. I buy myself one and continue towards the shoreline.

The whole conversation with Broc actually turned out to be a lot easier than I had anticipated. I'd felt mostly in control of myself and everything. But something about Broc's eyes has left me feeling strange. They're softer and inkier than they used to be. His whole nature seems softer too and much gentler. Perhaps Cassie is right. Broc does seem to have changed and it's not making my resolve to dislike him very easy.

Broc and I kissed once. Well, actually, it was me that kissed him. It happened a long time ago.

Mother and father had thrown a big ceilidh on the estate. I was about sixteen or seventeen, and had helped myself to a glass or two of Bucks Fizz or Lambrini, or whatever that low-alcohol, fizzy stuff was called. The bubbles had somehow emboldened me and given me courage.

I remember that I'd seen Broc standing outside. He was alone, on the bridge, just staring at the loch. I'd gone over quietly and stood next to him. His older brother, Shane, had just died a few weeks earlier in a car accident and Broc was sad.

Broc leaned his elbow on the railing and turned to look at me. I'd been shocked to see that his eyes were glistening from emotion as if he were about to cry.

With Broc's arms on the fence and his head leaning forwards, we were eye to eye, the same height.

That was when I went for it. I'd leaned in and kissed him.

He didn't react. Nothing. He just let me finish and then, pushing his elbows away from the fence, he stood up straight, standing tall above me once again. I can remember expecting him to say something. I waited anxiously for him to either reject me, or to sweep me up into his arms and kiss me again, but he didn't do either. He didn't do anything.

Andy had then appeared and the moment was over. Embarrassed, I went back inside and left them together talking. I felt like such a fool.

In all the years that passed, Broc never spoke to me about that kiss. It's something that has never been mentioned between us.

I should have realised in that moment that he'd never choose me. If I had, I could have saved myself years of wishing and hoping.

As I look out across Loch Ness, I again find myself feeling very much alone. I long to have someone beside me who will wrap me into their arms and give me the comfort I need just now. I've been in one or two relationships over the years, but none of them ever lasted longer than a few months. They were all nice guys, but none of them were Broc. Even when I'd kissed them goodbye at the end of a romantic date, my thoughts had been on Broc. It wasn't fair to do that to someone and so I'd broken off each relationship in turn. That's why I'm still single and alone.

With a sigh, I realise that my thoughts are drifting away from the point in hand and so I pull them back to the conversation that Broc and I have just had.

I know now that I don't think Broc was the one who murdered Andy. I never really have thought that, not even when the police told me that a lot of the evidence pointed towards him. I think back over that supposed evidence and wonder if it had just been based on the words of Will, who it seems is clearly lying about something.

And then there's Ailish. I'm shocked by what Broc has just said about her.

As I stand idly throwing pebbles into the loch, something truly terrible occurs to me. The possibility of it travels through my nervous system like a shot of electricity.

If something had been going on between Ailish and Andy, and if Will had reason to believe that Lily was unhappy, then that didn't give just the two of them a motive to kill. I feel my legs trembling as I realise that it gave Lily a pretty big motive too.

My legs are trembling so much that I have to sit down. The small pebbles on the beach are damp from the earlier rain, but I don't care. I shakily lower myself to the ground and pull my knees in towards my chest.

Is Lily capable of killing her own husband? Out of everyone, her mental state is the most suspicious. I feel a stab of pain in my heart at the thought of it being possible.

What was it Inspector Shaw had said to me? He'd told me that he was sure that someone was lying.

Is William lying to cover for Lily? After all, the bullets in her rifle had been tampered with and his prints were on her gun.

Or, worse still, is Lily lying about her amnesia? Is that a bluff and can she actually remember everything? Had she lied when she told the others she shot a deer? Had she in fact seen very clearly what she had taken such a perfect, clean shot at? Is that why she's refusing to see me, because she knows that I'll be able to detect the truth?

Shaking my head, I take my phone out from my pocket and unlock the keypad. Flicking through the hundreds of photos in my gallery, I eventually find one of Andy and Lily's wedding. My eyes sting as I look at it.

It had been a perfect day in every way. It was the fairy-tale wedding that they had both deserved. Andy and Lily's love story up until then hadn't been simple.

Even as little children, Andy had been sweet on Lily. Lily was like a delicate doll, and he wanted to take care of her. Andy, Broc, Lily, Will and I had all attended the same primary school in the village, and we spent our holidays playing together on the estate.

Then they'd all moved up to the secondary school in Inverness. It wasn't until a year later that I was old enough to leave the primary school and join them. All the girls at school liked my brother. He was good-looking and kind. He was sporty and popular. It wasn't just the girls in Andy's school year that liked him, younger girls did too. Most of them were my friends.

I met Ailish at secondary school. We were in the same set for most of our classes and we hit it off instantly together. We had the same humour and were both a bit geeky in our own ways. When we discovered that our fathers both belonged to the same hunting syndicate, it cemented the friendship.

Ailish was one of my friends who liked Andy.

Most of the time, I didn't mind, but now and again it would really grate on me when she went on and on about him. It also affected things with Lily too. You see, despite the attentions of half the school, Andy only had eyes for Lily. Ailish is a really good person and has many, many good qualities but she also has one ugly flaw: jealousy.

I view jealousy as something ugly because I've seen how it can make someone, who is normally of a meek and mild personality, behave completely out of character and perform actions of a menacing and malicious manner.

One day, when I was just thirteen-years-old, Lily walked into the lunch hall at school, and I could tell instantly that she'd been crying. Her eyes were puffy and swollen. Ailish, who was sitting next to me, wore a smug smile on her face as Lily tearfully told me that someone had ripped up all her assignments and cut holes in her sports kit.

Ailish never admitted that it was her, but I knew it was. Her disappointment at how sad I felt in Lily's behalf was what had given it away. She'd miscalculated my feelings and that was the only part of the whole thing that made her show any compassion or feeling.

Ailish was jealous of Lily for two reasons. Firstly, because Andy loved Lily. And secondly, because Lily and I were close. I know people say they have a best friend, but I have two. I genuinely do. Both Lily and Ailish are my best friends. At least they were back then, before it all changed, and Andy was killed.

Lily and Ailish were both so different in their personalities, but I loved them both equally. This was something that Ailish found hard to understand. After a year or two she came to like Lily and the two of them got closer. We became an inseparable trio, although I've always wondered if I was the filling that held the sandwich together.

We went from being teenagers to young adults, and Andy was everything you'd expect of the son of a Scottish Laird. He was well mannered, confident, fair in his dealings with others and good with investments. Our own father had been a man of a very similar character.

Sadly, there were many who disapproved of Andy and Lily's match, including father. We were told that it had caused uproar in the family, and also in the village, on the day that father had returned home with his English wife. But, over time, our mother had won the hearts of everyone who came to know her. Father had refused to be won over by Lily though. He liked her as a person, but not as his potential daughter-in-law and the future mother to the next generation of McClintocks.

Lily came from a working family and, worse still, a family that worked on our own estate. Father wouldn't permit them to marry, and he and Andy fell out badly as a result. It pained me to watch them as their relationship cracked and split apart. I looked up to my father so much and I loved my brother dearly. I wished for years that they would just see eye to eye on this. Father pushed Andy towards other, more suitable women, one of whom was Ailish, but Andy made it clear that he wasn't interested.

Ailish didn't seem to be particularly put out by Andy's rejection though. By that time, we were a lot older, and she had lost her obsession with my brother and even been in and out of one or two serious relationships of her own. Although none of them ever lasted until a marriage proposal.

Following father's death, Andy quickly made Lily his fiancée and then his wife. I'd never seen a couple so in-love. She doted on him and would do anything for him. And I've never seen a man swaddle and care for a woman the same as I saw Andy look after Lily and her delicate ways. They were perfect together. Perfect, that was, except for one upsetting problem.

It plagued Lily that she couldn't seem to fall pregnant. Having waited so long to marry, she was determined to start a family as soon as possible once they were wed. Andy, also keen to carry on the McClintock line, was eager to have a few bairns running around, but they didn't arrive. Everyone told Lily to be patient and assured her that children would soon come along, all in good time. I think Lily tried not to be concerned, but as the months went by, she got more and more wound up over it and, within a year of their wedding, it had become a bit of an obsession; one that played with her fragile mind.

However, from what I understand, they'd begun to seek help from the doctors just a few weeks before Andy

167

died, and Lily was feeling much more settled and hopeful as a result.

I think back to the video call Andy had made to me on that fateful morning. They had both seemed so happy together.

I turn the screen of my phone off and their faces disappear into darkness.

My stomach is still a ball of knots from thinking about what has been implied by the things Broc told me. I'm beginning to question everything I've ever known and believed about my brother. I've always thought of him as the essence of goodness, but perhaps I was wrong. Perhaps he was really a master of deception and I never truly knew him at all.

And then, from nowhere, a brief, fleeting memory comes back to me. It's from the morning of the hunt. It's a memory of my phone call from Andy. I can see him now, the hesitation on his face after he'd asked me whether I'd spoken to Ailish recently. Was there something he'd wanted to tell me, to admit to me, but not had a chance to as he was interrupted by George entering the room?

I know that I've resisted contacting Ailish since I arrived in Scotland, but I've now come to the conclusion that it's maybe time to get in touch with her. I need to know what it was that had been going on between her and Andy. I need to know the truth.

28th December 2020
3:53pm

Ailish was frozen. The sun had set, and the light was now fading. She was about to pack her things away when a movement to her right caught her eye. The area was overgrown with small ivy bushes and other shrubs. She lifted her thermal imager to her eyes to see what was there.

Ailish watched as the white outline of a single, solitary deer moved about. She put the imager down, picked up her binoculars and focused them on the animal. She wanted to be sure. Focusing in, she could see it was a hind. The animal was slowly picking her way through the woodland ahead. She was fairly close too, within a hundred and fifty yards of her seat.

Ailish had been shooting since she was a teenager. Her father had been a close friend and shooting companion of the late Mr McClintock and, with no sons, he'd insisted that his only daughter learn the skill too. 'Ailish is a natural,' her father had sworn to everyone, and it was true; she was. She'd won various competitions and shot countless impressive beasts.

Leaning her head forwards, Ailish looked down through the scope on the top of her gun. She located the hind and just followed her for a moment. Ailish liked to get a good look at the animal before she shot it. She liked to admire its beauty first. There was so much undergrowth though, that she couldn't really see her properly to admire her.

Then, the creature stepped into an area with very little foliage. Ailish smiled. She was beautiful. Her dark, reddish fur was more of a greyish colour with its winter coat. She looked healthy. She would eat nicely.

The hind put her head down for a moment to pick at the ground and Ailish took a second to steady herself in preparation. Then, as the deer lifted her head, Ailish,

169

confident and sure of her aim, released the safety, drew in a steady breath, and pulled the trigger.

The bullet glided smoothly through the air, faster than the eye could see, and Ailish watched, having pulled her binoculars swiftly back up to her eyes, as the deer dropped instantly to the floor. She listened for a moment as the birds took off into the sky, but nothing else moved.

Ensuring that her gun was safe, Ailish made no move to go and check her kill. Instead, she put the rifle down and sat back in the seat, listening to the sounds of the forest around her. She felt tears stinging at her eyes as she wondered if she'd ever hunt with her father again.

Considering the Future of Balnair

It proved to be hard to get hold of Ailish. She took a whole day to reply to my message and then didn't finalise a time to meet me until four days later. At first, I felt impatient with her lack of haste, but she said that although she was extremely busy, she was also grateful that I'd got in contact, and so I tried not to be too annoyed.

Today is the morning of the day I'm going to see her. We've arranged to meet later this afternoon at the waterfalls down the road for a 'walk and talk'. Again, as with Broc and Dores Inn, the place is on neutral ground which I feel is needed.

I'm sitting in the office with George and we're going over some of the paperwork for the estate. It's actually our third morning of doing this. It's something that needed doing and I'm grateful for the excuse to hide inside for most of the day. I've been trying to avoid bumping into either Lily's father or her brother before I get a chance to speak with Ailish. After my talk with Broc, there are plenty of questions that I'm eager to put to William, but I'm anxious to get to the bottom of Ailish's story first.

I never realised just how much is involved with running the estate. I've always been grateful that we have George and for everything he does, but this process of going through the paperwork is giving me a new appreciation for him, on a different level.

Most of what we have been through and discussed is good news. Both my father and Andy had evidently been great businessmen, with a good eye for investments and incredible organisational skills. The bank accounts are healthy, and the losses so far have been minimal. Everything is currently running well. I'm well aware though that nothing has been done regarding the business side of the estate for over nine months. George has explained to me that there is only so long that a machine can run itself without some new fuel being injected into the system.

This is where I feel out of my depth. Unlike my father and brother, I have no eye for financial opportunities and my skills for organising a Highland estate are nowhere near on a par with theirs.

There is also the issue of what I personally want to do with everything.

Do I want to live here, running the estate?

I've considered this question countless times since Andy died. His will made provisions for Lily to remain in her home, but everything has been left to me. It's something our father had stipulated in his own will that would happen in the event that Andy should die childless, as he sadly had.

I try to picture myself: the spinster landlady, caring for an older mother and a slightly mad sister-in-law, whilst rattling around this big, old family home. A home, I have to say, which will then remain empty following my own death as I shall have no children of my own to inherit it. It's not a particularly bright prospect and often those thoughts end with me desperate to rent everything out to some trust, or investor and disappear back to Oxford. Back to my small, happy little flat with my simple, no-stress job.

But then the thought of running back to Oxford leaves me feeling sick too. The thought that I might possibly hand my beautiful Balnair over to some organisation or entity that will manage it, but never love it as I do, is just as hard to stomach as the idea of dying here alone.

The truth is, I have no idea what I really want to do.

Each evening, I watch my mother and can't bear the thought of causing her the distress and upset that I know a move from her home would do to her, should I decide to give it all up. Each afternoon, I walk Buddy along the side of the loch, and I feel a warm glow inside as every nerve in my body absorbs the beauty and magic of the familiar scenery that has surrounded me for the past week. And, each evening, I sit and look through the albums of old photos and am reminded of the long family history that the McClintocks have in this part of the Highlands.

George and I have just been looking together at a folder of research on wind turbines. We already run a small hydroelectric scheme from the loch, but there is scope on the estate to harness more natural energy. A large wind farm, run by one of our neighbours and already well established, is situated further along the valley and George has informed me that Andy was intending to install a handful of turbines on our own land. Apparently, he had felt confident that the revenue they would bring in would not only pay for the installation costs quickly, but also set the estate up with some extra guaranteed income for many years to come. The estate is large, and the house is big. There are estate staff salaries to pay and, of course, mother's ongoing care to think of. Income is needed.

'Broc still rents land from us for grazing, doesn't he?' I ask George, whilst trying to understand the jargon inside one of the packages from a company promoting wind power as a source of income for landowners.

'Aye, he does,' confirms George. 'But it's not enough to keep this place running.'

I drop the brochure I'm reading onto my lap and rub my forehead with my hand. George looks at me.

'Did you see young Brochan the other day, Miss?' he asks. George is trying to sound casual, but I can tell from his face that he's worried by something.

'I did,' I admit openly. 'We had a drink at Dores and a talk about things. I had some questions that I needed to ask him.'

George nods. I think he understands.

'Brochan Henderson is a good laddie.'

I smile faintly and think back to how open Broc had been and how he'd spoken honestly with me about everything. 'He is,' I agree, and frown a little as I realise that I mean it.

'Do you... do you think he did it?' George asks. His voice is hesitant. He's clearly not sure if he's overstepping his place by what he's asking.

I blink and shake my head slowly. 'No,' I reply. 'No, I don't think I do.'

I hear George breathe a sigh of relief.

'But, speaking to Broc has left me with lots of questions,' I continue. 'I'm meeting with Ailish later to ask her a few things.'

George now looks up at me sharply. 'Are you sure you're okay with this? Going around talking to them all? Raking the whole thing up again and again?'

His eyes are filled with deep concern, much like a look that I'd seen in my father's eyes many times when I was younger. I feel touched that he cares and almost choke a little.

'I need to do this,' I answer him, kindly but firmly. 'I need to get to the bottom of it and know the truth.'

George looks away and I watch as he moves a few bits of paperwork about. Then, after a moment he speaks again. 'Is this whole situation affecting your feelings towards the estate?'

I sense my skin heat a little in response to his question. 'What makes you think that?'

'The other day I turned the computer on in here and it was open on the page for the National Trust for Scotland. I guess that with you settled in England, it might make sense that you'd be thinking about giving the place up.'

I don't answer and George continues, 'I know you've fallen out of love with the Highlands, and I suppose that with everything that's happened, it must be a dreich place for you to be. I'd probably be considering leaving too, if I were you.'

I find that I have to blink hard as my eyes begin to sting behind my eyelids. George has discovered what I've been considering, but he's drawn all the wrong conclusions about why.

'George, I've not fallen out of love with the Highlands.' My voice is shaking. 'I love the Highlands and I love Balnair more than anywhere else on earth.'

George looks at me for a moment. He's obviously relieved to hear that I love this place, but then his brows knot together again.

175

'Then why are you considering giving it all up? That's what you're doing, isn't it?'

I sigh. 'To be honest, I don't know what I'm considering,' I say. 'You're right, I do have a bitter feeling about staying here, but it actually has nothing to with what happened back in December. It goes back further. It's complicated.'

'But you think that all these questions will help with that?'

'Not really,' I reply with a small shrug. 'I'm asking the questions because I want to know the truth.'

I drop my eyes back to the brochure about turbine investments and pretend to continue reading it. But my mind is far away. The skin on my face prickles a little as I realise that the small amount of time which I've spent with Broc may have already helped with my bitterness more than I'm ready to admit.

Getting to the Deep Stuff with George

'About knowing the truth...' I say, looking back up to George who is still watching me, concerned. 'I know we spoke a bit the other day about everything, but I still have more questions and I'm wondering if you can shed any light on some of them.'

'I dinnae know what answers you think I might have, but I'll do my best,' he says, his face now pale.

I take a deep breath.

'I'd been gone for almost a year before that awful day,' I start to say. 'A lot can happen in people's lives in that amount of time, and I know the pandemic put everyone under strain.' I hesitate and George waits patiently for me to continue. I decide to just say it straight. 'Do you think that Andy and Lily were unhappy?'

'No.' George looks shocked by my question. 'Why would you say that?'

I swallow down a small lump in my throat as I remember that I have, not one, but two reasons to think that something wasn't right between my brother and his wife. Which reason should I give to George though?

I decide that the letter is private, and therefore not mine to talk about. What Broc saw though, that was public and so I can mention that out loud without feeling like I'm talking out of line.

'Broc thought there might be something amiss between them,' I explain.

'How so?' asks George. He doesn't seem to be aware of what I'm about to say.

'He said that he saw Ailish and Andy embracing... closely.'

'When?' asks George. This news seems to be completely new to him.

'The day before the hunt.'

'Does young Brochan think there is something more to it than just friendship?'

I nod and George puffs out his cheeks as a sign of his disbelief.

'Well,' he says. 'That explains the mood that Brochan Henderson was in that day.'

I look at him. 'So, Broc was angry that day?' I ask.

'Aye, but I didnae know why.'

I turn cold as my mind processes what George is saying. Inspector Shaw has never removed Broc as a suspect.

George and I sit in silence for a while. The clock on his desk ticks noisily. It's the only sound in the room. Finally, I speak again.

'What do you think happened to Broc's missing deer?' I ask.

George looks at me and closes his eyes for a moment. When he opens them, I can see that he wants me to explain more before he gives me an answer.

'Inspector Shaw told me that they never found his injured hind. He said that without that deer it looked suspicious on Broc's part, that he could have actually shot Andy, not a deer.'

I can't believe that I'm now going over this, after having told Broc just a few days ago that I believe him. It's like

I can't settle my trust in anything.

George answers my question with a question of his own, 'Who is to say that we didnae find his deer?'

He can see the confusion on my face, and he continues to explain, 'There was a wee injury on the front leg of the dead deer we found next to Mr Andrew. Inspector Shaw assumes that the injury we found on the deer that day was from Miss Briars' shot. What if it was actually from Broc's?'

I ponder this for a moment and then slowly begin to understand what George is saying. He is implying that the dead deer was injured first by Broc, and not by Ailish. That would release Broc of suspicion. However, it puts either Lily or Ailish to the top of the list. With two gunshots remaining, it would mean that one of them killed the deer and the other one killed Andy. With the two things happening so close together, it would be easy for either woman to blame the other and release themselves of suspicion by doing so.

I shake my head. No matter which way I turn and which new discovery I make, I don't like the potential truth that faces me. Despite my questions and searching, each of my friends is still a potential killer.

I think for a moment of each one of them and the different flaws in their characters that could have given a motive to kill.

Ailish: my best friend. Did Andy perhaps not give her something she wanted? In the past, I've seen her behave in a cruel manner due to jealousy. Is she capable of such a thing now, despite being a grown adult?

What about Broc: the guy I've loved my whole life? He was Andy's best friend. Could it be that his sense of justice got the better of him when he thought that Andy had behaved deceitfully to, not only him, but also Lily?

Or Will: Andy's brother-in-law. He's quirky with his autistic ways. I've seen him hold grudges and respond with violence in the past. Did he overcome his fear of guns enough to take it upon himself to fight on Lily's behalf?

And then there's Lily: Andy's devoted wife and my sister by marriage. She's sweet, innocent and fragile, but did something make her crack and pull the trigger on her own husband?

'Miss Laura? Are you okay?' I jump as George reaches out and places his hand on my shoulder.

For the past few days, I've been trying to recall the exact words of Inspector Shaw during one of our phone calls. They now suddenly ring through my ears.

'At least one of them is lying.'

What he meant was that more than one of them could have done it. There could have been a murderer *and* an accomplice.

I narrow my eyes and look at George. Suspicion is again threatening to overtake me. Could George have collaborated with one of the others? Broc maybe? Or even Ailish?

'Miss Laura, my wee lassie, is everything alright?' he asks again, and I realise that I haven't answered him.

I shake my head a little, frustrated that my thoughts are so out of control.

'Yes,' I reply, looking into George's kind eyes.

'Get a grip, Laura,' I tell myself. *'There's absolutely no way it's George.'*

'You looked a wee bit lost,' he says, still visibly concerned.

He's right. I am lost. I'm lost in this mind-numbing hunt for the truth, but hopefully a chat with Ailish will put at least one thing straight for me.

DCIS: So, it was a surprise when Mr McClintock showed up at your seat that afternoon, was it?

AB: It wasn't a complete surprise, as he'd told us all that he planned to come to see us, but aye, in that moment, it was a surprise.

DCIS: How long did he stay at your seat?

AB: Only a couple of minutes. Maybe five at the most.

DCIS: What did you talk about?

AB: Not much.

DCIS: I asked what you talked about.

AB: It's personal.

DCIS: This is a murder investigation. Personal or not, I need to know what you talked about.

AB: As I said, it's personal.

DCIS: Are you refusing to answer that question?

AB: Aye. At this moment in time, I am. It has nothing to do with Andy's death and I'd rather not say.

DCIS: Miss Briars, how close were you and Mr McClintock?

AB: I would say that Andy was one of my closest friends. Laura, his sister, is my best friend and we're all a close group. We've hung around together for years: Broc, the Mitchells and us.

DCIS: Was there anything about your relationship with Mr McClintock that you would describe as closer than a platonic friendship?

AB: No! Why would you ask that?

DCIS: We have a witness who says they saw Mr McClintock and you embracing tightly just the day before he was killed. Can you explain that to me?

AB: Andy had been helping me with some family issues and a few other things. I was a bit upset when we met, and he was just giving me a hug. That must be what your witness saw. He gave me a shoulder to cry on for a moment, that's all.

DCIS: So, you were embracing someone, outside of your household?

AS: Aye. I'm aware that goes against the Covid rules but, as I said, I needed a shoulder to cry on.

DCIS: If you're saying that you were not involved with Mr McClintock romantically, can I also ask, if there was any reason for you to be upset with him, or to carry a grudge of some sort?

AB: No. Andy was just a really good friend. One of the best friends someone could ask for.

DCIS: Okay, back to when he arrived at your seat...after speaking with you for a few minutes, Mr McClintock was heard on the radio. He apparently said that he was going to walk towards Mr Henderson's seat. Is that correct?

AB: Aye, it is.

DCIS: Did you see him walk in that direction?

AB: No. As soon as he stepped down from the seat, I went back to looking for deer.

DCIS: Mr McClintock's body was found very close to your seat. Is it possible that he stayed close by to your seat and was shot by someone there?

AB: I'm sure that I would have seen him if he had hung around the area of my seat.

DCIS: Did you at any point see Mr Henderson nearby?

AB: No.

DCIS: How did Mr Henderson appear to you that day?

AB: I barely spoke to him, but he was quieter than usual. I think something was bothering him.

DCIS: Do you think he was upset with Mr McClintock in some way?

AB: I doubt it. They were best friends.

DCIS: You said in your statement that you took your shot late in the afternoon, moments before dusk, is that correct?

AB: It is. I was about to pack up, when a movement in that area caught my eye.

DCIS: Miss Briars, you live in Inverness, is that correct?

AB: Aye.

DCIS: How often do you go hunting?

AB: Until the start of the pandemic, I was hunting regularly. At least a couple of times a month.

DCIS: And I understand that you are an experienced hunter?

AB: I am. I first began to hunt as a teenager. I don't want to brag, but I've won a few competitions.

DCIS: How confident are you that the target you aimed at on the 28th of December was a deer?

AB: Very confident.

DCIS: Please explain to me why you're confident?

AB: Because I am. I can't explain why. I checked the imager and the binoculars. I'm confident.

DCIS: Do you have any comment about the fact that Mr McClintock's body was found in the same place you claim to have aimed at, and taken your shot?

AB: No, I don't know what to say about it.

DCIS: Mrs McClintock's range from her seat also covered that area, didn't it?

AB: Aye, it did, but only just. It would have been a

long shot from her seat.

DCIS: I understand that she has a good aim though?

AB: Aye, she does, that's true.

DCIS: Do you know if Mr and Mrs McClintock were happily married?

AB: They were really happy.

DCIS: Does Mrs McClintock know the details of the personal matter that you and her husband were discussing, moments before he died?

AB: No, she doesn't.

DCIS: Does she know that her husband was offering you comfort when you were upset, the day before the hunt?

AB: I don't think so, but you did say that someone saw us.

DCIS: I did. Miss Briars, do you think that Mrs McClintock could have had a reason to be upset, or even angry with her husband?

AB: I suppose she could have been upset. But if you're trying to insinuate that she would have killed him, then you're wrong. Lily wouldn't ever do anything like that. They really were in-love.

DCIS: Miss Briars, in my experience, the most common motive for murder is love.

Face to Face with Ailish

I'm in Foyers again. A complete week has now passed since I arrived back home. With thoughts of wind turbines on my mind, I'm sitting in the car. Eileen and I are parked in the small public carpark, next to the village store, waiting for Ailish to arrive. Again, I'm feeling nervous. It's not a pleasant experience that I seem to be putting myself through, that of facing people who had once been close friends but who are now distant acquaintances. However, it's all part of something I need to do.

I see her car arrive and she parks up a few spaces away. Anxiously, I make my way over to meet her.

Ailish gets out. Her slim, long legs, swing slowly from the driver's doorway. She pulls a cardigan out from within the car and throws it around her shoulders, flicking her long, dark hair out from underneath. She's facing the other way and so hasn't seen me. I'm convinced that my stomach must be breeding butterflies as I step closer to say hello.

Ailish turns around and I try not to let my face reveal the shock I feel inside. She looks terrible. Ailish, who has always been slim, has lost a lot of weight. Her pale skin hangs over her cheekbones, making her appear gaunt and ill. She doesn't look like my old friend.

'Thanks for coming,' I say awkwardly. As determined as I've been to remain stoic until I know the truth, I feel my mouth turning upwards in a sympathetic smile.

'I was happy to,' she replies, also smiling. Although her smile is more wary. 'To be honest, I've barely set foot outside the city all summer. It's a nice change to be away from the brick and stone.'

She pops her sunglasses over her eyes, and they hide the heavy, dark circles that I've already noticed.

'Are you okay?' I ask gently. Despite my misgivings about her involvement with my brother, I still feel a flutter of concern for my, one-time, best friend.

She sighs. 'Life! It's been a rough year.'

As I watch Ailish shrug her shoulders, I realise that I know nothing of what is going on in her life. I feel a sudden stab of guilt. When I left Scotland, twenty months ago, I allowed myself to drift from Ailish. It wasn't for any reason other than my own selfishness. It was difficult for me to leave my beloved Highlands behind when I ran away from Broc and his wedding. Contact with Ailish was a painful and constant reminder of everything I missed and so I gradually let the communication, and the friendship along with it, slide. Then, after Andy died and she remained a suspect, I found that I had no desire to speak to her. Something now tells me that I've behaved badly and as a result, I'm not exactly sure how I should conduct myself.

'Shall we walk and talk?' she asks, and I nod in response.

We cross the road and follow the pathway that is signposted towards the falls. For a minute or two we walk through the woodland in silence. Ailish leads the way with me following just a few steps behind as we weave our way past small families of tourists. Finally, it feels like we've escaped the masses and we begin to follow the steep, zig-zagging steps downhill.

'Do you want to tell me about your year?' I ask, and Ailish stops walking to look back at me. I'm standing two steps behind her and, for once, it is as though I'm taller than her.

'I thought you asked to see me because you wanted to talk about Andy,' she replies. She sounds tired.

'I do,' I answer. 'But you sound like you've had other things to deal with too. I just thought that if you wanted to talk, then, well...'

Ailish nods at me gratefully.

'Things have been far from easy,' she says, as she begins walking again. 'Father had a stroke back in September last year. It was serious. He lost all the use of his right-hand side, and his speech was badly affected. It meant that he had to stop work.'

I don't say anything, but I feel terrible. I hadn't even known.

Ailish continues, 'I thought that everything would be okay. I assumed that dad, being a high-flying businessman and that, would have a decent pension and insurance, but I was wrong. Mother and I were shocked to discover that he had nothing. He didn't have any sort of security net for us in place at all. I had to take on his business or risk it going under. On top of that, in February, I was diagnosed with cancer.'

I gasp.

'It's okay,' she assures me. 'They've caught it quickly and are confident that it's not spread, but I've still had to do a load of radiotherapy and everything, so it's taken a lot out of me. Thankfully, I avoided chemo, and so didn't lose my hair.'

We stand to one side to let a couple climbing up the steps towards us come past. Once they have gone, we begin to walk on again.

'I'm so sorry. I didn't know any of that had happened,' I say, my voice sounding meek and apologetic. Ailish doesn't say anything in response. 'How is your father now?' I ask, fearing what she might say.

'He's in a nursing home.'

'Who is paying for it,' I wonder out loud.

'I gave up my flat in town and mother sold their place. We've moved into something smaller together. The profits of the house are paying for the home, but they won't last long. When the money runs out, they shouldn't be able to claim it from us or from the house we now live in as it's in mother's name only and therefore not an asset belonging to father. I may have to sell his business though. Or, you never know, a miracle might happen, and he'll get help from the benefit system or something.'

'Are you still running the business?'

'I'm trying to,' she shrugs. 'Although I have no idea what I'm doing and absolutely no energy either.'

We've reached the upper viewpoint for the waterfall and Ailish leans on the railings to take in the view. I stand alongside her.

The Falls of Foyers are in front of us, dropping one hundred and sixty-five feet below. Although not as wild and full as it can be after heavy rainfall, the white cascade of water is beautiful. The sound of the rushing water is both exciting and calming at the same time.

'I'm really sorry. I should have known. I've been a rubbish friend,' I tell her. My voice is quiet against the backdrop of the falling water.

Ailish doesn't protest against what I've just said. Neither does she try to correct me, and I know that she thinks me to be a rubbish friend too.

'So, I presume you want to ask me all about what happened that day?' she says, changing the subject. She sounds weary, like talking about the hunt and everything is the last thing she wants to do.

'I do,' I admit. 'But actually, I need to get to the bottom of something more important than that.'

She turns away from the view and looks at me.

'What would that be?'

A family of tourists have joined us at the viewpoint, and I wait until they've continued on down the steps before I answer her. I feel hesitant and guilty to be firing accusations at her after everything she's just told me, but I tell myself not to give in to excuses. I need to know the truth.

'Was something going on between you and Andy,' I ask, getting quickly to the point.

'What do you mean?' she replies, her voice is cool and calm, but I can't help noticing that she shuffles uneasily on her feet.

'Broc said that he saw you both, the day before it all happened. He said you were in an intimate embrace.'

Ailish's face turns an even whiter shade of pale and I'm sure that Broc had definitely told me the truth.

'Laura, don't tell me you think that Andy and I were... that we...' She stammers for a moment and then her manner becomes angry. 'Tell me, Laura, what exactly do you think? What sort of low opinion do you have of me, and of your own brother too?'

I'm now lost for words. *'What do I think?'* I ask myself.

'I suppose, it just seems to me that there might have been something going on like, maybe... well... to be honest, the word 'affair' does come to my mind. But it doesn't seem like you or Andy would do that. I'm just confused and need to know what was going on.'

My eyes are stinging and I'm willing myself not to cry. I can't, not here, not like this.

Looking at Ailish's face, it's clear that she's still annoyed, but then her expression softens as she sees how upset it's making me.

'Laura. Andy and I would never have had an affair. You do know that, don't you?'

I nod, not trusting myself to speak and wait for her to continue talking, to explain more to me. As I stand, watching her, the sound of the cascading water rings louder and louder in my ears, Eventually, Ailish continues speaking.

'Andy was consoling me because I was upset. I was just in the process of trying to deal with dad's business and getting him into the home. Andy met with me to give me money. He'd been helping financially for a few months. It was money that mum needed to pay the bills until I could sort the whole mess out.'

Bringing the Sheep off the Mountain

'So, that solves the mystery of the money that Andy was withdrawing from his account,' I explain to Broc.

It's the day after I met with Ailish and I'm filling him in on what we'd spoken about.

The two of us are walking down the mountain which overshadows the back of the house. It's late afternoon and we're bringing the sheep down from the hills. All the groundsmen for the estate are nearby. It's something we always do at this time of year. We'd hiked up the mountain after lunch and then sent the dogs off to round the flocks up. Our sheep and Broc's are all grazing on the wild, moss-covered land. Today, they're being brought down to the lower area around the loch to graze for a few more months before winter.

'Why didn't Andy tell anyone about the money?' asks Broc, having already listened carefully to everything I've told him.

'Ailish had made him promise not to. She said her father and mother are both very private and it would have been humiliating to have others know that they were facing financial problems,' I say, climbing over a large, stony outcrop.

'I can't believe that my last conversation with Andy was bitter and full of accusations that I now know were wrong,' says Broc. His voice cracks a little and I can see that his eyes are full of tearful regret. Shaking his head, he quickly changes the subject.

'How did you and Ailish leave everything?' he asks.

'We had a hug. I told her that I'd like to try and get back to how we used to be, when we were close. She said that she wanted the same; but it will take a while, I know it will. I wasn't the friend I should have been when she needed it,' I reply, honestly.

'All of us will take a while to get to where we used to be,' says Broc, stopping for a moment to retie his bootlace. I watch him. I can't believe that after all this time and after everything that has happened, we are now up on the mountain together, talking calmly to each other. It's both strange and yet normal at the same time. He stands back up and looks at me. The intensity in his eyes is too much to bear and I have to look away.

'Do you think that you and I will ever be friends again, like we used to be?' he asks.

I still can't look at him and so I focus instead on the sheep. 'I hope so,' I reply, but I'm not sure how convinced I sound. So many of my old feelings for him are stirring and I'm finding it hard to keep them under control.

We keep walking as we're moving the sheep forwards, ahead of us, and Broc speaks again. 'I have a feeling that the distance between you and I started long before December the twenty-eighth, last year. You cut me off many months before then.'

Instantly, heat burns on my cheeks and I know that my face is red.

Before I can respond to him though, there is a sharp whistle and George hollers at us. Half a dozen sheep have separated from the others and are running past us towards the hedge line. We've both lost focus on the task at hand.

'Blast!' curses Broc and shouts for his dog. While he runs off to reclaim the escapees, I retrace our steps up the hill slightly, attempting to block them from retreating back the way we've come. Obediently, Broc's dog follows his master's instructions and soon the six breakaways are back with the rest of the flock.

It's a noisy crowd that we're escorting down the hillside. Hundreds of bleats are singing an inharmonious chorus which echoes around the mountains.

We walk over the brow of the hill and the loch comes into view. It's glimmering in the early evening sunlight and we both pause for a moment, taking in the view.

'What will you do with this place, Ginge?'

Broc's words throw me. It's a subject that has been on and off my mind all week and yet I still don't know the answer to that question.

I suddenly feel a need to keep my cards close to my chest. Our conversations together over the past few days have allowed him to get closer than feels comfortable. I sense that we're possibly re-bonding far too quickly with each other and this is now my opportunity to regain a bit of control over everything.

'I'm looking into options,' I reply, trying my best to sound nonchalant about it.

We have begun to walk again, following the mass of woollen creatures that are descending from the hillside, but Broc now stops walking and looks at me.

'You're not seriously thinking of returning to Oxford, are you?' His voice is full of shock. 'You don't belong in Oxford.'

'Oxford is my home now,' I say, with a small shrug, as I

try to keep my voice cool in an attempt not to betray the knots that I feel inside.

'No, it's not,' he insists. 'You belong here. You're a Highlander. You're not a city kind of girl. I don't believe that you think of Oxford as your home.'

'Well, you should,' I reply, as my voice trembles a little. 'I'm settled there, and I've made a new life for myself over the past year or so.'

Broc looks away and carries on walking, whistling instructions every now and then to his dog.

As I follow him, I think about what I've just said. I want it to be true, but, as I consider everything and everyone back in England, I realise that there is actually little truth in what I've claimed about Oxford. My flat is lovely, and I have made it my own in a way, but it doesn't really feel like home when compared to Balnair.

I think about my regular walk home from work. Each evening I usually cross Magdalen Bridge. Often, I like to stop and lean over, just watching the gentle ebb of the water for a minute or two. It's nice, but it's not like returning to Balnair. Over the past eight days, each time I've rounded the corner and seen the loch, I've felt a warm, glow inside. Each time I've stopped and paused the car on the bridge and then looked down at the rushing river, I've been filled with a contented, happy feeling. There is a certain sentiment about returning home that I wish doctors could bottle and give out as a prescription to people when they're feeling anxious and unsettled. I've taken that feeling in many times over the past few days and it has done me the world of good.

We're close to the fence line and the gateway to the loch itself. The sheep have reached a bottleneck. They're all trying to squeeze between the fence posts towards the fresh grazing ground beyond. Broc and I stop to stand guard, looking out for any that might now bid a hasty retreat back up the mountain. We're both silent, but then Broc begins to speak again.

'I didn't really appreciate you before,' he says. His voice is quiet against the noise from the sheep, and I hold my breath as I listen to what he's saying. 'You'd always been 'Andy's wee sister', but the truth is, I really missed you when you left.'

I have to look away.

'I mean it. I'm not joking,' he says.

Broc thinks I've looked away because I don't believe him. But the truth is, I do believe him. Ever since I got back, he's had a strange look in his eyes when he's either been talking to me or listening to me. It's a look I've seen many times towards other girls, girls that he'd been sweet on and taken a fancy to. It's definitely not a look I've ever seen aimed at me before.

'I guess I've missed you too,' I admit.

'You never replied to any of my messages after you moved away,' he says. His voice sounds hurt, and I wince a little.

'No,' I reply. I feel guilty, but I'm not about to explain the reasons why I'd cut him off. I can't tell him about the pain I'd felt that he never chose me. He'll think I'm foolish.

'It's just, I think I may have taken our friendship for granted,' he continues, ignoring my lack of explanation.

I look back at him and something about his eyes awakens an excitement in me. I'm sure I can detect a touch of desire in the way he's watching me.

He opens his mouth to add more to what he's saying

but, before he can speak, a movement beside the loch catches our attention and we both glance away to see what it is.

Looking down, I can see that Will is walking along the side of the loch. He's carrying his fishing rod. Will looks up at us both and I'm sure I see him scowl. All thoughts of Broc and his soft, desirous eyes disappear as another subject pushes itself forward.

'Did Ailish say anything to you about what she thinks might have happened that day?' asks Broc, as if reading my mind.

I swallow the lump which has formed inside my throat at the sight of William.

'Yes,' I reply. 'Ailish said that she thought there was something suspicious about the way Lily and William behaved at the end of the afternoon, especially once you'd all discovered Andy's body. She suspects that one of them, or both of them, knows something that they're not saying.'

'Well, I think I agree with her,' says Broc.

I think of Lily and turn to Broc, shaking my head.

'No. Not Lily,' I tell him. 'I spoke to both her and Andy that morning, and I'd never seen them look happier.'

I look up at the sky as my thoughts are carried away by the memory of Andy's face on my phone screen. When I lower my eyes, Broc is no longer looking at me either. He's turned back to face the loch. I follow the direction of his gaze and my eyes rest again on the solitary figure that is walking along the water's edge.

'If you ask me, William Mitchell is the one you need to still talk to. He's definitely hiding answers to something,' says Broc.

I shudder as I realise that he is right. Tomorrow, I need to find Will and talk to him.

28th December 2020
4:00 pm

Andy was definitely on the trail again. The drops of blood on the ground were heavier. The injured deer must be slowing up in her movements.

He'd heard a shot a few minutes earlier. It was hard to tell where it had come from, but it seemed to be close.

The light was now fading, and Andy glanced up. He'd been so focused on tracking the injured hind that he'd lost perspective of where he was.

He looked about.

He knew this woodland like the back of his hand, but now he wasn't exactly sure of his location.

He cursed himself. He wasn't sure if he had a working radio and he was now putting himself in danger. He took a moment to get his bearings and his inner sense of direction told him that he wasn't far from Ailish's seat. He knew that he needed to be careful.

Andy checked his watch. He'd told them all to stop at 4pm, so hopefully they would be packing up now.

He paused, trying to work out what to do.

On one hand, he wanted to find this deer, but on the other hand he knew he was at risk. He had no torch and no radio.

Fairly sure that he was closer to Ailish's seat than any others, he decided to walk towards where he thought her seat was, keeping to the cover of undergrowth as much as he could.

No one would risk firing at an obscure, unidentified target.

<u>Looking at Photos with Mother</u>

It's been a long afternoon, bringing in the sheep, and now I'm tired. I quickly heat up some left-over food from the day before and take it through to mother's room to eat with her. She's already eaten her meal and is settled on the settee. Julie has got the photo albums out as usual.

'I'm sorry I'm late,' I say and head straight over to sit next to mother, balancing my bowl of hot pasta on my lap. Buddy pads over and sits in front of me with his eyes fixed longingly on my dinner. I ignore him. I don't believe in sharing human food with dogs.

Mother doesn't look at me but instead continues turning the pages of the album. Julie gives me a kind smile from across the room.

Having finished one album, mother picks up the next. I instantly recognise the tight, red curls of my brother in the first photo, and so lean over to look more closely. The photo must have been taken when he was about five or six. He's in his school uniform and carrying an oversized rucksack on his back. He has a huge grin on his face and his eyes are shining brightly.

I blow cool air onto my steaming forkful of food and watch as mother's fingers run softly over the photo.

I'd give anything to know what's going on inside her mind: to know what, if anything, she can remember about the events surrounding the photos that she looks at each evening.

I continue eating my food under the watchful eye of Buddy. A ribbon of slimy drool is beginning to fall from his mouth, and I push my legs against his chest, shoving him aside. Mother is now muttering faint, almost inaudible, words.

I pop another forkful into my mouth and look over again to see what it is that she's looking at and talking about.

She's staring at a photo of us children. It had been taken in the snow and there are sledges in the foreground. Again, mother's fingers are running across the page.

'That's Lily and Billy, the twins,' she murmurs, and I glance sideways at her, surprised.

'That's right,' I comment. My fork is held, poised in the air as I swallow the mouthful I'm eating. All my attention is on mother as I wonder just how much she can remember.

Her fingers move to the next child.

'Brochan Henderson,' she says, her voice barely above a whisper. 'He's a little scamp, that one.'

I stifle a chuckle. That's an accurate description of the little boy that Broc had once been.

Mother's attention pauses for a moment on my brother who is holding onto his sledge and smiling at the camera.

'My Andy.'

I again feel that familiar burning sensation of many un-cried salty tears against my eyes as I watch her. I'm not sure if she ever thinks of Andy during her strange, day to day existence, but to see her now showing this recognition of him touches me greatly.

My eyes flick ahead to the next person in the photo. It's

father. He's wrapped up in his big coat, standing just behind Andy. He's holding something in his arms. Or rather, someone. Squinting closely, I can see that it's me. I must have been about four years of age. My arms are clinging tightly around my father's neck. I can't remember that day. It's one of those memories that is from a time when I was too small to recall it. Miraculously though, my mother seems to be able to remember who we all are.

'Our Lil,' she says. 'Little Laura Lil.'

Her words are so quiet and yet, they hit my ears like a clap of thunder.

The clang as my fork falls from my hand and clatters onto the china bowl makes us all jump.

Mother's face looks frightened by the sudden noise and Julie jumps up from her seat in surprise. The bowl then slips from my lap and Buddy leaps at it, eager to eat its remaining contents.

I lean forward to pick it up, but my hands are shaking and trembling.

Julie reaches out instead and removes the bowl from where it has fallen. Buddy continues sniffing around at the floor, cleaning up all the remnants of my tomatoey pasta.

'Is everything alright, Miss Laura?' Julie asks.

'Yes. Yes,' I reply, staring again at the photo. 'I'm sorry. Clumsy me. It's been a long day,' I apologise.

'You don't need to stay here if you're tired,' says Julie, kindly. 'Your mother is quite content. Feel free to go to bed if you need to.'

I nod.

'Yes. I think I will, if you don't mind,' I say, gratefully.

After taking a deep breath to steady myself, I stand up from the settee and leave the room as calmly and quietly as I can.

Once in the hallway, all appearance of calm disappears as I scramble up the stairs and rush my way to my old bedroom as fast as my legs will take me.

Mother just referred to me as, *'Little Laura Lil'*. It's a name that had been lost in the recesses of my mind. Lost that is, until now. Everyone had called me Little Laura at one stage, but it was my father who would slide the two words together and create the name, 'Lil'. That was his special, pet name for me since the day I was born, but then, as I started primary school and we'd become better friends with Will and Lily, I'd insisted that I didn't want to be called 'Lil' anymore. So, the name 'Little Laura' was replaced with my current name of 'Wee Ginge'. My father went from calling me 'Lil', to 'Winge', and I forgot all about that funny, old name that he used to use. I forgot, that is, until mother just said it, a moment ago.

My shaky legs eventually carry me to within reach of the chest of drawers and I pause. There's a mirror on the wall in front of me. I look at it. My reflection stares back at me. My eyes are wild, and my skin is pale. Lily had put those letters in my set of drawers because they're mine. They belong to me.

What was it William had said when I'd gone to the cottage? *'You never wrote to me'*. I'd thought it odd at the time, but, of course, it made sense now. He'd been writing to me the whole time. He'd sent letters to the house via Angus, the postman. Angus had commented that it had been a bit confusing, and I suppose it would have been. He'd have been given a letter addressed to

'Lil' and been told that it was for Laura. He, like me, must have assumed the letters were for Lily. Maybe Lily had even thought the same at first. Perhaps that was why she had opened the first one, before realising that I was, in fact, the intended recipient. That must be the reason why she'd stored them all in the bottom of my chest of drawers. The letters had been kept there for when I would return home and read them.

My legs are still shaking and so I kneel down on the floor and take the small bundle of envelopes out from the drawer.

I take a moment to reread the first one again. Its words now make more sense. Will had obviously worked out that I'd left because I was upset with Broc. He'd seen me crying that day, out by the loch. Will wrote that he loved me. I can't help but let out a sigh as I realise that he probably does. He's always followed me everywhere, looking for ways to get my attention and approval.

I slowly make my way through the other letters. They're all fairly short in length. Will wrote about the fish in the loch and how he wished I'd come home. He complained that I wasn't replying and told me about how Lily would send food down to the cottage for him and his father. The letters are innocent, childish almost. They remind me of the old style of letters we used to write to a penfriend when we were at school.

I get to the last letter and open it carefully. Unfolding its pages, I see the same neat writing and my name at the top.

Dear Lil,

Something happened but I can't tell you what. When you

hear about Andy you will be sad. You will cry. It makes me sad that you will cry, but I'm happy too because I hope that soon you will come home.

I know you don't want to come home, but it will be okay. I have taken care of him. You can come home, and you won't have to see him. The police will soon take him away.

Lily is very sad. I think she is ill. If you come home, you can look after her. You are good at looking after people. I hope you come home soon. I miss you.

B

I turn the page over and examine it. Like the others, there is no date, but I already feel sure that I know when this letter was written.

I put the letter down and stare at the floor. My mind has gone blank. So many thoughts that should be whirling around have been pushed to the side and a black empty space of nothing is left.

Could Will have really done it? Will was innocent and afraid of guns, but he also held onto grudges. Was he so in love with me that he'd do something like that to get rid of Broc? Had he been holding a grudge against, not only Broc, but, also against Andy? Had Andy, stressed out from the pressures of the pandemic and the burden of helping Ailish and her family, snapped out at Will, thus moving Will to respond in an action this violent? Or had he, like Broc, thought that Andy had been cheating on Lily?

As I sit and ponder everything for a moment, there's one thing that stands out to me. It's something I've always known about Will: he'll do anything to protect the people he loves. That's when my mind settles and I feel certain that I've discovered the truth.

The high-pitched call of a Screech Owl pierces outside the window and I look up to see that it's dark outside. I then realise that I'm extremely tired.

Picking up the letters, I leave my old bedroom and make my way to the room where I'm sleeping.

Without brushing my teeth, I get straight into bed. Closing my eyes, I lay my head on the pillow and will myself to fall asleep.

28th December 2020
4:31 pm

Will hurried back to the seat and to his bag.

After he'd accused Broc, his instinct was to run, even though it meant abandoning Lily back there.

His thoughts were racing. He felt confused and everything was unclear. He needed to make sure that they believed him. He needed his story to be true.

He looked around and saw that Lily's gun was in its slip, next to her bag.

He needed to make it look as if her gun hadn't been used. He thought that if he made sure that all the bullets were in the gun, then they would think that no one had fired it.

Will's hands shook as he took hold of Lily's rifle and slid the bolt handle back. He hated guns. They made him nervous, but he'd watched Lily load her rifle several times. He could do this.

He took the magazine out and then went into her bag for the bullets. He grabbed one and pushed it into the empty slot. He wasn't sure if it was the right way round, but there was no time to check. The others would be back soon.

Still shaking he replaced the magazine and then put the rifle back down where he had found it.

Scared, and feeling sick, he decided to just run home. He could hear the others coming. Will took one last desperate look around him before he turned his torch off and then ran, stumbling through the darkness towards the small cottage that he shared with his father, at end of the loch.

<u>Discovering the Truth</u>

Reaching out my hand, I pick up my phone to look at the time. It's 6.15am.

Almost two hours have passed since I last looked at the time. For the first night since I arrived back at Balnair, I've been plagued by my old companion: insomnia. The night has been long and full of distressing thoughts, wakeful moments and the odd snippet of a nightmare. Broc's face also flashed up frequently during those long, dark hours. Strangely, his rugged features had been the single, comforting thing to pass through my subconscious mind all night. At one moment, the Laura that was existing in my dreaming state had snuggled against Broc's chest and felt the warmth of his strong arms around her, but then she had caught sight of Will. He had been holding a smoking rifle in his hand, and she had immediately handed the strange illusion over to the real world. I'd once again awoken with a start, feeling restless and covered in sweat.

As I sit up and lean back against the headboard of my bed, I'm relieved that the morning has arrived. I can at last surrender to this fight with sleep and get up.

A glance in the mirror tells me that I look terrible, and so I take a shower and put on some makeup, attempting to hide the shadows beneath my eyes.

I'm eager to go immediately, but there's no point. It's still too early. Instead, I force myself to try and eat some breakfast. I just about manage half a slice of toast with some strawberry jam spread on top.

After pacing around for another thirty minutes I decide

that it's a reasonable time to leave. I walk out the back door and make my way towards Eileen. As I open the door and get in, I notice that even she has failed to make me smile. I feel that there is nothing that can possibly lift the mood that today is bringing with it.

Taking a moment, I check my phone one last time before leaving the WI-FI signal behind. Still nothing. I'd emailed Inspector Shaw in the middle of the night, telling him that I need to talk with him at the station as soon as possible, but it's still early. He probably hasn't picked up his emails yet. He will though. And when he does, I'll hopefully be ready to see him.

As I pull out of the driveway, I take a quick look at the loch. My eyes rest for a moment on Will. He's down on the far shore, fishing. He looks up and waves, but I don't wave back. I can't find the strength to lift my hand off the steering wheel. I hesitate for a moment. I need to talk to Will, but not yet. I shall talk to him later. *'He doesn't know that I know,'* I tell myself, as I continue driving down the road. *'I need to get to Lily first.'*

Arriving at New Craigs Hospital as the morning sunlight is beginning to bring a warmth to the air, I make my way over to the reception and ask to speak with Doctor Fraser.

'Miss McClintock, I wasn't expecting to see you again so soon,' she says, greeting me.

'No,' I reply, trying my best to maintain my composure. 'Something has come up and I absolutely have to see my sister-in-law,' I explain.

'I'm sorry but as you know...' begins the doctor.

I interrupt her. 'Yes, I know she has said not to see me, but this really can't wait,' I insist. 'I have a note prepared for her. Could you please give this to her? I think she'll agree to see me if she reads it.'

I hand Doctor Fraser the note I'd written earlier, and she reads it. I expected that she would. She raises her eyebrows as she reads the words I've written to Lily.

Lily, darling,

I must speak with you. I'm fairly sure I know what William did, and why he did it. I have to tell Inspector Shaw what I know, but I must clarify things with you first. I know this will be hard for you to talk about, but I'm always here for you.

All my love,

Laura

'If she agrees to see you, I will need to be present too, her mental health is our priority,' says Doctor Fraser.

I nod and she disappears down the corridor with my note in her hand.

After an anxious, fifteen-minute wait, she returns and asks me to follow her. We make our way to the ward where Lily is staying. As we walk into Lily's room, I'm relieved to see how lovely it is. It's warm and cosy. It's everything that a person recovering from a distressing mental illness would want a room to be. I'm glad that Lily is here. This place feels peaceful, and I know that it's an environment she will need after today.

Lily is sitting on a sofa in the corner of the room. Sunlight is flooding through the windows and onto her pale, drawn face. Her eyes are wide and scared and she's looking at me fearfully as I enter the room.

I decide to take control of the situation and so I go over and sit beside her, hugging her immediately. Lily's body feels stiff, and tight in my arms. As I hold her, I hear her sniff. She is crying.

'It's going to be alright,' I whisper and then sit back in the sofa and look at her.

She won't make eye contact as she takes a tissue and blows her nose.

'Must I keep my face-covering on?' I ask Doctor Fraser who is waiting by the door.

She nods.

I turn again to Lily. I'm here now. I was worried that she'd still refuse to see me, but she hadn't. Now we need to talk.

'When I got home last week, I found the letters that Will wrote to me after I left,' I begin.

Lily looks at me, confused.

'You put them in my chest of drawers,' I explain.

She nods and I continue talking. 'I thought they were for you, and so I didn't open them. But then last night I realised that they were for me and so I read them. The last one told me everything I need to know.

Lily looks away. I can see that she's petrified, but I have to keep going.

'I think that there are two people that Will loves very much,' I say. 'He loves you, of course. But I also now realise that he loves me too. The thing is, William's feelings are not always rational like ours, are they? He wants to protect the people he loves.' Lily looks back up at me and nods.

I take in a deep breath. This is hard. I can see the fear in Lily' eyes and I wish that I could just snap my fingers and make it all go away but, after all this time, I'm sure that I now know the truth and it's important to put this whole thing to bed. Breathing out slowly, I carry on.

'I don't know if you remember, but Will told the police that it was Broc who killed Andy. I think he said that to protect the people he loves. I don't think he knew how wrong it was to tell a lie like that. He thought that it would protect me from being upset anymore over Broc and... well... he was protecting you, wasn't he?'

Lily's eyes begin to fill with tears and so I reach out to take her hand.

'The thing is,' I say, keeping my voice as gentle and loving as I can. 'You were just as confused as the rest of us, weren't you? You couldn't remember anything from that afternoon.'

Lily shakes her head fervently.

'I honestly couldn't remember anything. Not a single thing!' she says, her voice surprisingly strong behind her frail features.

'But a couple of months ago, you started to remember, didn't you?' It's a guess, but I'm sure I'm right. It would make sense, the changes that had happened in Lily's behaviour and communication with me. She nods and I know I've understood what happened correctly.

'Lily, I wish you'd called me when you started to remember. I'd have been here in an instant to help you. You've been suffering for months by yourself, holding this terrible secret in.'

The tears are now rolling down her eyes.

'I wasn't sure if it was memories or nightmares to begin with,' she sobs. 'But I soon realised that it was, in fact, memories returning to me. The first memory that returned was of that moment when I saw him, lying on the ground, in a pool of his own blood, with that brown hat of his still on his head. Next, I began to recall the moment I took my shot at the deer, but the images of Andy wearing his hat kept haunting me. That was when I started to guess at what I'd done. But I still wasn't sure what was the truth as I'd been so confident that it had been a deer in my sights. I didn't know what to do with my suspicions. I felt like tearing my hair out. I tried to ask Will once, but I couldn't bring myself to say it. I didn't want my fears to be true. That's when I think I went a bit mad and lost my grasp on reality.'

I can picture Lily, alone in the big house at Balnair, tortured by the memories that were returning to her, too scared to talk to anyone about it for fear of what would happen to her. No wonder she'd slowly gone mad. How she must have suffered. I feel a hot tear fall down my own cheek and I brush it aside.

'I wish you'd called me,' I tell her, as I once again wrap my arms around her.

'You must hate me,' she mumbles, her voice shaking between sobs. 'I was so foolish to attempt such an unclear shot at such a stupid, ridiculous distance. I'm sorry. I'm so sorry. I loved him so much.'

Lily's voice again breaks up and I hush her gently whilst stroking her head. Tears are flowing freely down my own face too and I can't stop them.

'I don't hate you. How could I ever hate you? I know you loved him. And he loved you too. It's okay. It's okay,' I say, trying to soothe her.

As I'm holding her tightly, my heart almost breaks for this woman who is my best friend and sister-in-law, and for the turmoil of emotions that are washing over her. I glance at Doctor Fraser. She is visibly concerned, but still allowing us to continue talking. Her face looks worried and I can see that for her this is all a revelation. Lily obviously hadn't told the nurses or doctors here about her memory recall either.

Gradually, Lily's sobs lessen, and I feel her relax slightly against me. It's as though a huge weight has been lifted from her, now that she knows that I know the truth. Then I feel her body stiffen again and she turns to me and grabs hold of my arms.

'You said that you're going to see Inspector Shaw. What will happen to me?' she asks, wildly.

'Lily, you mustn't be scared,' I soothe. 'Inspector Shaw will understand. It was an accident.'

Lily put her flask back into her bag. She'd offered Will a drink, but he'd said he was okay.

'I'll come down then,' she whispered to him. The light was rapidly disappearing, and it was gone 4pm. Andy had told them to stop about now.

Just as she was about to get down from her seat, Lily saw a movement far away, to her left. She squinted. There it was again. It was a long way from her, over three hundred and fifty yards away at least, but something was there. It was big enough to move the bushes about.

She lifted her binoculars to her eyes, but it was no good. There was a lot of foliage, and the light was too low to see anything clearly.

Lily took her thermal imager back out from her bag, having already packed it away. She looked through it, scanning the area where she'd seen the movement. It was hard to see but there was definitely something there, moving about slowly in the foliage. The white shadow of the body heat showed up through the imager, obscured here and there by leaves and branches. It was big. It wasn't a fox. It was taller, much more like a deer. It had stopped moving and so Lily picked up her rifle and placed it back on the ledge in front of her. She pulled the butt into her shoulder, placed her hand against the fore-end and looked though the scope.

Where was it? It had moved. She carefully scanned the area and located it. Again, it was partially obscured behind foliage and bushes, but she could clearly make out the brown top of its body.

If she got this, then it would be her furthest shot of a deer. Andy would be impressed.

Excited at the prospect, Lily took in a slow, deep breath.

Adrenaline was already beginning to build in her veins, and she knew that she needed to steady herself if she was going the make the shot.

The deer still hadn't moved. That brown patch of fur was lined up perfectly in her sights. She needed to take the shot now or it would move again, and she'd lose it.

Lily held her breath. She counted to three: one, two... On three she released the safety and pulled the trigger. It made her jump a little. It always did when she fired the rifle.

She couldn't see what happened but there was no rustling of the undergrowth. No flashes of brown and white as the hind ran away. Lily was shaking with excitement. She rested the gun across the rail and picked her thermal imager up again. There it was: a warm spot, a large, white shape on the ground. She'd hit it. She'd taken a nice clean shot at a distance of over three hundred and fifty yards. Lily felt herself shaking. She couldn't wait to tell Andy. Quickly, she packed her bag and made her way down from the seat.

<u>Six Months Later</u>

February 2022

Taking a sizzling pan out of the oven and closing the door, I then place it on the side. Wafts of hot, herby, chicken juices hit my nostrils and my stomach reacts with a small rumble. Tearing a tiny bit of crispy skin off the top, I pop it into my mouth and the tastebuds on my tongue explode.

There's a familiar pattering of paws and I look down to see that Buddy has come to investigate the smells which are coming from the kitchen. He sits nicely and looks at me hopefully, his tongue hanging out of his mouth.

'Sorry Bud, but this is definitely not for you!'

Hearing a hiss, my attention goes to the hob, where a pan of vegetables is boiling over. As I'm removing the lid and turning the heat down, the doorbell rings. It must be Ailish arriving. It's okay though, I can hear that Lily is going to answer it and so I focus again on the meal that I'm in danger of ruining, if I lose concentration.

'Hey, do you need a hand?' Broc has sneaked into the kitchen without me hearing him.

I feel his warm hand rest on my waist, and I squirm as he leans forwards and gives me a gentle kiss on the back of my neck. A tingle flows down my spine and it's hard to resist the urge to turn around and pull his face towards mine for more.

'Yes! You could cut the chicken for me. But don't

distract me or it will all be spoilt,' I reply, smiling and flapping a tea towel at him.

Broc gives me a soldier's salute and begins carving at the chicken, placing thick slices of meat onto a serving tray.

'And don't pick at it too much, there's a lot of us to feed for lunch,' I add, as I watch him throw a slice of meat into his mouth. He grins cheekily and continues carving.

Ten minutes later, we are all sitting around the dining table together. I can't help but take a moment to pause quietly and watch as everyone helps themselves to the food that I've prepared.

Mother is sitting to my left, at the head of the table. I've already dished her meal up and cut it into smaller pieces for her and she is eating happily. We still have a large care package in place for mother, but I've changed a few things. I've made sure that she has at least one meal a day with us. I feel that the interaction is important for her and I'm sure I've already seen some benefits as a result. Her eyes seem more engaged with things around her and less distant than they used to be.

'Do you like it?' I ask her, still avoiding calling her mother in order not to distress her.

'Yes, my dear. It's delicious,' she replies, and I smile. I never know if she's aware of who I am, but just having this normal interaction with her is something to be grateful for.

Opposite me is George. He's piling his plate high with food, as if building a mountain. It makes me happy. He's never married and so never had a woman to cook a good meal for him. I find it satisfying to feed someone like George. He's been wonderful since I arrived home back in August.

The initial plans for the turbines are now being submitted and he's taken care of everything. It has allowed me to support the others throughout the court hearings. To be honest, I don't know what I'd have done without him here, keeping all the cogs of Balnair turning.

Sitting beside George is Ailish. She's pouring herself a glass of wine. She catches my eye and smiles. Ailish is looking well. Colour has returned to her face, and she's gained a few pounds. Once the truth was out, I spoke to George about Ailish's situation, and he was able to find a position on the estate for her. It's mostly admin, with a little bit of publicity work for some of the schemes that we are hoping to get involved in, but it's an opportunity to continue supporting her family situation whilst dignifying her and not making her feel like a charity. Andy had been right to give her money when he did and I'm glad that we can continue to help her. Our friendship has been rekindled and I value her company so much.

Next to Ailish, and opposite mother, at the other end of the table, is Lily. Her demeanour is still fragile and frail, but she's getting stronger each day. The police and lawyers worked closely with the medical team and were extremely kind throughout the whole legal process. It had all helped Lily greatly. Those who gave their reports in the courtroom discussed sympathetically the unfortunate, and slightly negligent, choices that Andy had made that afternoon, with regard to his own actions. They made mention of how Lily, without any radio contact from her husband, would have never expected an experienced hunter to be standing in an area that was within her range of fire.

It was almost a year to the day of Andy's death when we heard the coroner give the verdict of 'death by misadventure' and the inquest was finally closed.

Everyone involved could see that it was just a tragic accident and had wanted to put the whole matter to rest as quickly and quietly as possible. The balance between doing everything correctly and taking care of her both mentally and emotionally was struck in a way that I'd never dreamt possible. It had been good for all of us. I'd found it more distressing than I thought it would be, to hear the details from Lily's own mouth of how she'd shockingly pulled the trigger on her own husband without realising what she was doing. It was a traumatic few months for us both, and everyone else, but I feel that we are now healing.

The staff at the New Craig's Hospital looked after Lily expertly once they knew that her amnesia had resolved. They treated her for Post-Traumatic Stress and helped her to find ways to cope and deal with her ongoing intense grief and guilt. Eventually, six weeks ago, they deemed her fit to return home, whilst still monitoring her progress closely.

Lily originally told me that she would move out, but I refused to let her. She's family and I love her. I feel that we both need each other.

I'm still watching Lily, when Broc laces his fingers between mine and squeezes them gently. I stroke the back of his hand with my thumb in return and turn my head to smile at him as he is laughing at something George is saying.

Broc's laugh is infectious. It's like a roar that comes from deep within. His eyes are shining, and he looks so handsome wearing the shirt I bought for him earlier this week.

We've just celebrated a small, one-month anniversary together. Yes, that's right... Broc and I have officially been boyfriend and girlfriend for one whole month! I have to keep pinching myself to make sure it's really true, but it is. Broc is mine, at last.

Broc told me that he was in love with me the day after I spoke to Lily. You could have knocked me over with a feather at the time, but I could tell instantly that he was serious and that he meant it. He wasn't joking. He told me he'd realised that he loved me the moment I told him I was moving to England but had felt obliged to go through with his wedding to Jessica. When I never contacted him after it all went wrong, he assumed that he'd missed his opportunity and resigned himself to that fact. I didn't know it at the time, but Broc's confidence had taken a big hit when Jessica left. The old Broc would have driven to Oxford and told me immediately. Broc's quite different from the guy he used to be. He admitted that it took him a while to get back on his feet, but I soon realised that I actually love this new Broc even more than the old one. He's gentler, like a real 'Prince Charming'. He's perfect.

We took the first few months slowly, keeping everything quiet until the court hearings were finished, but once it was all over, and normal life began to resume, we made it official, and I don't think I've ever felt happier.

Everyone has finished eating and whilst the others are clearing the table, I put my coat on, whistle for Buddy and step outside for a few minutes. We walk down the driveway and within seconds he's found a stick and I'm throwing it for him. Reaching the bridge, I stop walking, lean my arms against the railing and look down the loch. The tops of the mountains are covered in snow and the water is still and glassy. Perfect reflections are resting upon the surface.

My eyes move to look along the track. I know Will isn't there, but I still look for him all the same. Hopefully it won't be too long before he can return home.

The judge and the members of the jury were kind to Will. Yes, he was found guilty of 'obstructing the course of justice', but they realised that, because of his autism, he hadn't fully understood the gravity of his meddling and lying. They could see what a vulnerable person he really is, and they realised that he said and did what he did that day because he wanted to help Lily. Will didn't know for sure, but as soon as he'd seen Andy, dead on the ground, he'd guessed that Lily had most probably made a mistake. He was worried that she would be blamed and get into trouble for it and that's why he'd interfered in everything. Also, Will had guessed that I left Scotland because of Broc. As a result, his twenty-five-year long grudge with Broc gained intensity during my absence and that was why he'd easily told everyone that it was Broc who'd killed Andy. His fear of what might happen to Lily had prevented him from understanding how wrong it was to point the finger in Broc's direction.

Will was lucky. He had been let off with a very small sentence in a special facility for those with learning problems. From what I've heard, he's doing well with all the help he has been getting.

I don't feel any bitterness towards Will. How could I? He's Will; our Will. What he did and said that day was done because he thought that it would be for the best, and maybe it was.

His actions had originally pushed everyone apart, but now it seems that we're all closer than we were before. If he hadn't have said what he did, Lily may never have gone to the mental hospital, and I may never have had a reason to return home. What's more, I may never have decided to take on Balnair as my own.

Something on the hill to my left catches my eye and I look up. There is a stag above me, beside the edge of the woodland. He's standing still, like a statue, just watching me. At that moment, there's a shout from the house and I glance away.

It's Broc calling me. 'Come on Ginge! Everyone is waiting to play a game.'

I look back to where the stag was standing, but he's gone, having disappeared into the forest of trees.

My thoughts instinctively go to Andy, and I feel a small lump form in my throat. Determined not to cry, I lift my hand to my mouth and blow a kiss. My breath sends it off to float down the loch. With a final glance around at my beautiful Balnair, I turn and go back inside to join my friends and my family, feeling confident that I'm going to get my 'Highland happily ever after', after all.

THE END

NOTE FROM THE AUTHOR

Aside from one childhood holiday, and a few weddings, I'd never really visited Scotland until September 2021.

I'd always been confused by visitors to the UK who would obsess over Scotland and its 'magic'. As far as I was concerned, there were plenty of amazing places they could find without having to venture so far north.

In the summer of 2021, my husband and I bought a roof tent for our truck and we set off on a 3-week long road trip. It wasn't many miles across the border from England before I began to understand what all the hype was about. Every corner presented us with a new view and yet another gasp of appreciation. I came to see what a stunning country Scotland is.

Whilst visiting friends in Inverness, we spent 2 nights wild camping at Loch Killin, which is where I have chosen to set Laura's home of the fictional 'Balnair Estate'. If you've ever visited Loch Killin, I'm sure you'll agree that it's a truly magical, inspiring place. We were 10 miles away from any phone signal and I loved every second of my time there (well, maybe not the moments when I was attacked by the midges).
It was during my first evening there that the ideas for *Hunting Beside the Loch* began and I formed a loose plot in my head. However, that was the easy part...

Writing a mystery and working out how to reveal things at a pace that keeps the reader engaged and guessing was hard. I went back and forth a lot. I hope I got the balance right and made it an enjoyable read for you.

I also had no idea about rifles or deer hunting. Thankfully, I had the help and advice of our friend Pete, who kindly spent time explaining things to me and even took me out on a mock deer stalk.

I hope that you enjoyed following Laura on her search for the truth and her search for what she wanted in life.

Although Laura bears very little resemblance to myself, I did add a touch of me to her character here and there. Her Covid anxiety is something I relate to, as do many, I'm sure. I also wanted to reflect in her the way I'd imagine I would feel if a place like Balnair was my home. Killin (the real Balnair) got inside of me within moments. I felt like it touched my soul. If you ever get a chance to visit, I recommend it highly.

I'd like to stress that while my descriptions of Balnair are based on the real-life setting of Killin, none of the details regarding the 'McClintock' family or the financial/business side of the 'Balnair Estate' are intended to bear any resemblance to actual people or places. These details are purely fictitious and were created within my imagination.

The real Loch Killin comes under the care of The Garrogie Lodge Estate which is owned by the Connell family. It was only after completing my first draft that I discovered the family on Google and learned what a huge contribution their estate makes to the local area. I read an article about the late Charles Connell from the Herald of Scotland and it was extremely interesting. It is my hope that one day I will be able to return to the Highlands, and perhaps meet the family who live in such an inspiring part of the world.

Hunting Beside the Loch was a break into something new

for me. My usual genre of writing is historical fiction and a 3rd person POV. I thoroughly enjoyed the process of branching into something new, contemporary and the ease of writing in the 1st person. I hope that you all enjoyed the results.

As with my previous books, I wouldn't have been able to get this one to the final stage of publication without help from the wonderful little team of friends and family that I have around me.

My mum once again played the role of chief editor. Her eye for detail made me check and double check a lot of the clues and red herrings, and she helped me to refine the plot into the story you have just read. The proof-reading team, who never fail to pick up on so many small mistakes, didn't let me down. Thank you again to Gillian, Beth, Amber, Teresa and Lianne. As always, my dad assisted me with the final formatting of the artwork.

I'd like to thank the loyal band of supporters that I seem to have gathered over the past two years. You know who you all are. You fly the flag for me, and give my books enthusiastic shoutouts. I really love you all for it.

If you have enjoyed reading this book, it would mean a lot to me if you would take five minutes to leave a review on Amazon (or Goodreads). I have chosen to self-publish my books rather than seek to find a traditional publisher and each review that my book gets helps other people to find it and then maybe decide to buy it.

Thank you.

Abigail

ALSO BY ABIGAIL SHIRLEY

After the loss of their parents, Myriam and her sister Rose drew closer together, supporting each other through life's ups and downs.

Now Rose is getting married and Myriam feels unsettled and anxious. However, an encounter with a mysterious stranger who works on the canal begins to dominate her thoughts and she finds herself falling in love. Myriam soon discovers though, that life doesn't always take the route planned as both sisters encounter obstacles to their dreams.

Will Rose's hopes of bearing children ever be realised? Will Myriam ever become the wife of the man she loves?

An absolutely beautifully written book set in beautiful surroundings. Abigail makes you fall for her characters and feel what they are feeling. It's heart-warming, heart wrenching and shows a true bond of two sisters. The book takes us back to simpler times which I loved.
-A Cracking Good Read

Will the lock Keeper's daughter ever find the Key to his heart?

ABIGAIL SHIRLEY

One Fine Lady

Twelve-year-old Becky has stopped hoping for any love and affection from her father. Her life alongside the busy canal in Banbury continues as normal until she travels to London, forcing her father to face reminders of what he once had but is now too afraid to embrace.

As Becky makes her journey from childhood into adolescence, she notices that something has changed. Should she open her heart and dare to hope again?

Like the horse drawn canal boats, amongst which this story is set, let yourself be pulled along by this family's story of love and loss.

I thoroughly enjoyed joining Becky on this heartfelt emotional journey. One Fine Lady is an insightful, pleasant, and well-researched window into the life of a small nineteenth-century English town. The diverse characters engender a spectrum of emotions ranging from joy, discovery, anger, sorrow, fear, and hope. Beware, your heartstrings will be pulled.
-DEREK J PACK

A stagecoach rolls away from Banbury, in Oxfordshire. Inside sits David, a young farmer with the world at his feet. He waves goodbye to his family and his beautiful, kind friend, Becky. Full of excited anticipation, David is bound for Chipstead, in Surrey, with a plan for his future and those he loves.

It's not long before he meets Amelia Armstrong. She's striking, charismatic and full of ideas for her own future.

Far away from home, and presented with new opportunities, David finds himself struggling to know what he really wants in life. He then begins to question everything he's ever hoped for. In the end, it comes down to what's most important and who he truly loves.

Will he pursue a different path, with new people and exciting prospects? Or will he set his heart on What's Been Left Behind?

The story captivates you straight away!

I loved every page!

Amazon reader

ABOUT THE AUTHOR

Raised in Oxfordshire and currently residing in Cornwall, Abigail Shirley loves the simpler things in life. After marrying her wonderful Cornish husband, her heart fell in love with his home county and in particular Bodmin Moor.

She enjoys walking, swimming, cycling and horse riding. The perfect end to a perfect day for Abigail would be sitting by a fire with a glass of red wine and some melted marshmallows, accompanied by a few close friends.

A vivid daydreamer, her mind often drifts away and she enjoys writing short stories and quirky poems as small gifts for her family and friends.

Hunting beside the Loch is Abigail's fourth novel.

Follow Abigail on Instagram @abigailshirleyauthor

Printed in Great Britain
by Amazon